You know what you've got a heart for when:

- Your friends tease you about a particular guy, and you feel your heart start to race.

- The guy himself asks you out, and your heart stops cold.

- The girls you're mentoring make your heart warm up.

- And, in the middle of all of it, you realize that your heart is nothing without God.

Books by Janet Tronstad

Love Inspired

*Dry Creek

JANET TRONSTAD

grew up on a small farm in central Montana. One of her favorite things to do was to visit her grandfather's bookshelves, where he had a large collection of Zane Grey novels. She's always loved a good story. Today, Janet is a full-time writer.

A Heart for the Dropped Stitches
Janet Tronstad

Steeple Hill®

Published by Steeple Hill Books™

STEEPLE HILL BOOKS

Steeple
Hill®

ISBN-13: 978-0-373-87487-3
ISBN-10:   0-373-87487-1

A HEART FOR THE DROPPED STITCHES

Copyright © 2008 by Janet Tronstad

Printed in U.S.A.

Keep thy heart with all diligence;
for out of it are the issues of life.
—*Proverbs* 4:23

This book is dedicated with love to my niece, Sara Enger. She is a woman with an open heart who meets life with joy. I am proud of her.

Chapter One

"As for you, my galvanized friend, you want a heart. You don't know how lucky you are not to have one. Hearts will never be practical until they can be made unbreakable."
—The Wizard of Oz, speaking to the Tin Man

I have always refused to let my heart be broken.

During one of the first meetings of the Sisterhood of the Dropped Stitches, our counselor, Rose, brought us this quote. We were just getting to know each other, but we already could see that we each had our own way of dealing with tears. Lizabett Macdonald, the youngest of us at fifteen, cried the easiest. Both Marilee Davidson and Carly Winston, the two oldest at nineteen and eighteen, would blink back their tears for as long as they could and then they'd let them fall. As for me, sixteen-year-old Becca Snyder, I never cried. Not ever.

The four of us were all teenagers when we got our cancer diagnoses, and everyone expected us to constantly

*spill our emotions and our tears. I hated that. I knew I
had emotions—the fear of death made that very clear—
but I had no intention of giving in to them, not even when
everyone started to think I really was the Tin Man.*

*In my opinion, we didn't need to dig into our feelings
and cry; we needed to figure out the rules to survive this
thing that was eating us alive. It was bad enough that
Rose had organized us into a knitting group; I refused to
go all girlie with the tears.*

I couldn't think when I was crying.

Seven years have passed since we first read that quote,
but right now the rest of the Sisterhood is staring at me
the way they did that night—like I, Becca, am their very
own personal Tin Man. Only this time they're all flushed
and proud because they think I've reached inside my tin-
man armor and found a heart beating with romance.

I wish it were that simple.

I carefully set down my knitting needles. We're sitting
around the table at one of our weekly Sisterhood
meetings and I need to set everyone straight on my love
life, or lack thereof. "Mark Russo is not my boyfriend.
Not even close. He's my boss. Big difference. The only
reason I mentioned how he looks is because of the girls."

I've learned over the years that most people don't see
things in black and white like I do, and I'm trying to be
sensitive to that. Sometimes I wish I could just follow my
heart, but I can't. For me, boss and boyfriend don't mix
at the best of times, and, with my life right now, I can't
see myself dating anyway. It's not that I'm worried about
dying or anything—all of the sisters have been official

cancer survivors for years now. No, the problem with me and dating right now is just my life.

The judge who is in charge of my summer internship is on vacation and so am I, but once she gets back in town, I will be super-busy—much too busy for even a casual boyfriend. Especially when I start law school this fall. I've worked too hard to get into law school to let it go up in smoke. That's the way I am. Logic always comes before emotions with me.

"He's not your boss. You *volunteer* at that shelter," Marilee says smugly as she sets down her knitting needles, too. At twenty-six, she's the earth mother in our group. She's warm and giving and so happy these days that her goodwill just overflows. She's in love with her boyfriend, Quinn, and she wants the rest of us to find true love, too. She probably doesn't even notice that I'm out of my league here. It's not that I don't want to find my true love; it's just that I can't seem to make the emotional connections.

"And," Marilee continues gleefully. "I've never heard you call any man handsome before."

"I'm just repeating what the girls say. That's all."

I volunteer at a homeless shelter for teenagers in Hollywood; I'm a big sister to the girls there. It's not as noble as it sounds. I started volunteering at the place several months ago because I needed a "good citizen" reference for my application to law school and working at the shelter seemed more interesting than picking up trash along the 210 freeway. I got my acceptance letter from Loyola Law School a week ago and have been planning my goodbye speech to the girls ever since. I haven't given it yet; but I'm just waiting for the right moment.

Of course, the right moment might find me quick enough after what I did today. My goodbyes might all be said for me with the wave of a pink slip. Come to think of it, I wonder if volunteers are given pink slips.

"Mark is enough of a boss that he can fire me." I don't need to get in touch with my emotions to figure that one out. "And he just might." I've finally worked my way around to the point of the conversation. "I broke the biggest rule in the place this afternoon, and he's strict with rules."

I'm twenty-three years old and getting fired doesn't scare me. What sends shivers down my spine though is that Mark might insist on updating the reference letter he sent to the law school admissions department. No aspiring corporate lawyer needs a piece of paper in her academic file that says she can't be trusted to obey the rules, especially when the rules apply to underage minors who are homeless. They are what's known as a *vulnerable population* in legal circles. Picking up trash along the 210 freeway is beginning to look more attractive all the time. At least there wouldn't be any way for me to torpedo my career.

"I can't believe you broke any rules," Carly finally says. "Your middle name is Rules. You live for rules."

I've always felt a little in awe of Carly because, if I'm the Tin Man, she's Dorothy with the ruby slippers. Everyone loves Carly, and I can't blame them. Carly is this San Marino girl with long, flowing blond hair and a face that makes guys turn around. I mean that literally. One-hundred-and-eighty degrees. I've seen it happen. And, it's not just her face. You just know you can trust her. People would line up to follow Carly down a yellow brick road even if they didn't know where she was headed. And I would be the first in line to follow.

I look at Carly now.

"Believe it," I tell her. "Because I broke the biggest rule in the place."

The four of us in the Sisterhood gather every Thursday night in a diner that Marilee's Uncle Lou owns. We moved on from fighting our cancer—me with my bone tumor, Carly with her Hodgkin's disease, Marilee with her breast cancer and Lizabett with the tumor in the muscle of her leg. And now we are trying to figure out how to fill in the holes in our lives that came from being sick for so long. Our old counselor, Rose, can't meet with us always, but the meetings with the Sisterhood are the most important part of my week. I think it's the same for the rest of the sisters.

Knowing they all understand me on the important things, even if they don't get me on romance, helps me make my confession. "I didn't set out to break any rules, you know that. It's just that some of the girls and I were washing the windows on the Melrose side of the building when a limo drove by. You should have seen the thing. The sunroof was open and this couple was standing up in formal clothes—you know, with the breeze blowing the girl's hair the way it does and the guy just leaning against the rim of the sunroof and grinning. He looked a little like Leonardo DiCaprio in a tux. Then the girl waved to us and the guy leaned over and kissed her. It was like a scene out of *Titanic*. Before the iceberg, of course."

Lizabett sighs. At twenty-two, she is the most romantic

of all of us. She takes ballet lessons and cries at the movies. She has a reddish tinge to her short brown hair and has taken to wearing it in a halo of curls.

I look around the table and continue, "You should have seen the look on those girls' faces when I said the couple must be going to their prom. Right away, the girls started talking about dresses and asking what it had been like for me to be a normal kid and go to a prom."

I lift my eyebrow at the others. They are starting to understand. We all know I couldn't tell the girls what it was like to be a normal teenager; none of us could except for Marilee. We had been sick instead of poor, but we had a lot in common with those homeless girls. Marilee is the only one of us who discovered her cancer after she'd graduated from high school. The rest of us had missed out on most of the usual things like our proms.

I swallow. "I told them, of course, about the cancer and how it was. But then I thought—why should they miss the prom like we did? It's not fair. There needs to be some justice in the world. There's no reason they shouldn't have an evening to remember. Not when they're healthy. So, I told them I would find them a prom to go to. Or something close to a prom with the clothes and the limo and the style."

"Wow," the sisters say in unison.

"I said it without really thinking," I tell them even though *that* revelation should not be necessary. Of course, I wasn't thinking. My knitting needles are on the table along with the ball of ugly beige yarn I'm using. I don't like the yarn even though it was on the free table at the yarn shop, and I was too practical to leave it there. It has been sitting at the bottom of my bag for months. Tonight I decided to pull it out. "So, that's what I did. And I can't back down. They trust me."

I wonder if anyone else is sitting here thinking that this is the reason why I shouldn't be allowed anywhere near my emotions. I'm better off as a Tin Man. When it's time for me to make decisions, I need to go with my head. I feel as miserable as that old ball of yarn. I should stick with rules. I understand rules. They work for me.

Of course, I know myself well enough to know it wasn't all sentiment that made me say I'd find the girls a prom. I've heard a lot of hard-luck stories, and I've never been moved to break any rules before. No, it was the injustice of it all that caught me up. It's not fair that some kids are always on the outside looking in. I don't want that for my girls.

"I don't suppose there's some way they *can* go to a prom?" Marilee asks after a moment. "Surely some of the kids at the shelter go to high school and—"

I look at her. "Believe me, no one there goes to high school. We're lucky if they go through the program we have for them to get their GED."

"Well, maybe one of the local high schools will let the kids go to their prom as guests," Carly says.

"I doubt it," I say even though I hate to always be the pessimist.

"Oh, there's got to be a way," Lizabett says.

Like I said earlier, Lizabett is sweet. She actually believes I'll end up on the Supreme Court now that I've got my acceptance into law school. I don't tell her, but I'm touched that she's my champion. I figure she balances me out in the universe somehow. You know, the yin to my yang. The flying optimism to my earthbound reality.

"Your boyfr—, I mean, your *boss,* Mark, will know how to get those kids into a prom," Lizabett adds with the blind confidence she sometimes has in people she hasn't even met. I happen to know she has a secret stash of superhero comic books and sometimes I think she's let them influence her too much. She continues, "All Mark needs to do is talk to a principal or someone."

That's like saying all Mark needs to do is turn into a superhero and save the world from destruction.

I no sooner think this then I remind myself that Lizabett is not alone. The girls at the shelter secretly think Mark is a superhero, too. That's how we got into this mess. I think he's the reason the girls are so caught up in dreaming about proms and limos. He's made them believe they're pretty enough to dream about things like that. Lupe, at fourteen, is missing a front tooth and Candice, only a year older, has a bottle scar on her left cheek. But Mark doesn't see those things and the girls forget them, too, when they're with him.

Plus, Mark has the kind of classic Italian looks that generally make a woman's heart flutter. Thick, dark wavy hair, warm brown eyes, a sculpted chin. Just the right amount of protective attitude.

I have to keep reminding the girls that just because Mark is single, that doesn't mean he would ever date anyone living at the shelter. He's not that kind of a guy. He doesn't even need to say he won't date anyone, it's just obvious. I don't bring up the age factor to the girls because they're a little sensitive about being young, but I know that's a double no-way for Mark.

I respect him for that. Well, that and the law degree he has from Harvard. He's not using it now, but he has it. I don't think the girls even realize what an accomplishment it is to graduate from Harvard Law.

When I'm around Mark, it's one of the few times I'm glad I have my Tin Man shell. Mark's a heartbreaker if I've ever seen one and I have no desire to wrap myself up in some romantic fog when I have my own law school to think about. I'm not planning to go to Harvard, but I'll need my wits about me at Loyola Law School, too. And a romance would only be a distraction. Not that I have to worry much about that with him anyway. It's hard to have a romance with someone who doesn't even talk to you except when politeness absolutely demands it.

"Mark's going to kill me when he finds out what I promised," I say. Like I've said, his protective manner has never extended to me. I know he won't smile and just forget this. Of course, he might talk to me a little more than he usually does. Not that he will be saying things I want to hear.

There is a grandfather clock in the corner of our room at the Pews, and I can hear the soft ticking as the others take in what I've just said. We smell coffee from the other side of the French doors that separate our room from the main dining area of the Pews. If I look through those French doors, I will see people sitting at tables and along the wooden counter that divides the space. Most of them will be eating one of Uncle Lou's hamburgers or drinking a cup of his signature coffee.

Finally, Marilee answers my unspoken question. "I don't think you need to worry about Mark being upset. You meant well when you said you'd find a way for the girls to go to a prom."

I swallow. "It doesn't matter. Mark says it's very important that we establish trust with the kids at the shelter. Sometimes a kid will run away if they feel like one of the staff has broken their word. I have to deliver. Fortunately, I said it would be something *like* a prom. It gives me some wiggle room."

"And, you're not staff exactly, either," Carly says helpfully.

"The kids won't see the difference in that. Besides, I have a duty to them."

"Well, then you'll find a way," Lizabett says. "Maybe we could pull out the phone book and find the numbers for some of the high schools in Hollywood. Someone's got to understand."

There's a moment of silence and then Marilee says, "Maybe we could pray about it first." She gives me a quick look. "If you want us to, that is."

I appreciate that Marilee asks and doesn't just launch into some prayer. This whole religion thing is a little difficult in the Sisterhood right now. When we first started meeting, I was the most religious one. Not that I believed anything about God particularly.

My religion is more about the family who has adopted me than anything I might believe. We are Jewish, but not observant Jews. My parents always make that distinction. I think they always say that so I will know that, even though I was born a gentile and adopted, I am accepted by them on equal terms. My parents and I don't want religion to divide us or to take too much of our time. In our family, being Jewish means that we celebrate the holidays together. Passover. Hanukkah. Sometimes we light the Sabbath candles. We often invite non-Jewish friends to share the holidays with us.

We don't expect much from religion. We certainly don't bow our heads and say a prayer before we eat—in public no less, which is what I've noticed Marilee and Carly do these days.

Still, I've been meaning to ask my mother why we never pray about things that are happening in our lives like Marilee does. Just so I'll be more informed. Our family prayers are all traditional ones, usually having to do with some past miracle from thousands of years ago. They seem more orderly than Marilee's bursts of prayer, but maybe a little dryer, too.

It's hard to figure out God.

I wonder what God thinks about all of these "help me, I lost my homework" kind of prayers that Marilee, and now Carly, pray. It seems a little strange to think that God would care about those little things. But I don't say anything. I'm not one to let religion come between me and my friends.

"Sure," I say to Marilee just to show that I have nothing against prayer. Or her God. Or her. Or the universe in general.

Carly reaches over to take my hand and that starts everyone grabbing hands until we have a circle of arms around the table. I like the circle part so I bow my head with the others.

"Father," Marilee begins. "We know how these girls feel about the prom. We know that You care about their hopes and dreams."

There is a knock at the French doors. Marilee pauses and then continues praying. "We ask that You show us how to help them. And help Mark understand why it's important. Amen."

After the prayer, we all look up. No one ever comes to the French doors when we are meeting except Marilee's Uncle Lou and he has already brought us our usual tea for the evening.

But Uncle Lou is back. He's standing on the other side of the French doors holding up a phone.

"Come in," Marilee says.

"Sorry to bother," Uncle Lou says as he opens the doors. "But I got a call here for Becca, and I thought it might be important."

"Me?"

Uncle Lou hands his cordless phone to me. "It's that guy from the shelter."

"Hello," I say into the phone. I already have a bad feeling about this. I never should have left the diner number as one of my contact numbers for the shelter. I make it a point to turn off my cell phone for the Sisterhood meetings, but the diner phone is always there.

"I need your help," Mark says, and I can hear the strain in his voice. I also hear lots of teenage noise in the background. "There's a rumor going around that you promised the girls they could go to a prom and I'm hoping you can talk to a couple of them and straighten it out. They must have misunderstood something you said."

I swallow.

"They're ready to have a fight over a bottle of nail polish someone left in the girls' bathroom," Mark continues, his voice tensing a little more. "They say they want to be looking good when they ride in the limo."

I clear my throat.

"I thought maybe you could talk to Lupe and Candice," Mark says. "They seem to be the ones going on about it the most. They can pass the word along to the others."

"I—ah—well, you see—"

I can feel Mark grow quiet. Don't ask me how. There is still all of that background noise, but I don't even hear him breathing.

"You didn't," he finally says.

I don't want to think about the disbelief I hear in his voice.

"It's really about justice," I say. "These girls need to feel like they at least get some of the same things that other kids get. Besides, it doesn't even really need to be a prom. Just a formal event of some kind."

I'm sure Mark went to his prom in high school, but I don't think it's tactful to bring that up right now. He probably went with a Barbie-doll kind of a girl, too—which should mean nothing to me, but somehow it does and it puts me off my rhythm so I can't think of anything to say for a second or two.

"Just where are we going to find this prom?" Mark finally asks. "Have you thought about that? We can't make the kids promises we can't keep. That's one of our main rules."

At least he doesn't remind me that I always preach to everyone that we need to follow the rules.

"Maybe one of the schools will let the kids go to their prom," I say. "The schools have a civic responsibility to do more than just help their own students."

Mark grunts in disbelief. "I can't even get any of the schools to let us use their gym for a basketball game. They're not going to let us crash their prom no matter how much we preach about civic responsibility. Remember, we have street kids. The schools are all worried about—I don't know what they're worried about—vandalism, drugs, disease, you name it. They've got a reason to worry about us."

I look across the table and see Lizabett looking at me. I don't think the others can hear Mark's words, but they're piecing everything together from what I've said. I can tell by the sympathy in her eyes that Lizabett knows.

I look away from Lizabett. Sympathy always makes me uncomfortable.

"We won't know that no schools will let them come until we ask," I manage to say. "Besides, it could be something else. A banquet maybe. Something like a prom."

Mark gets quiet again then he says, "Come to my office when you get here tomorrow. We'll talk about it then."

We say goodbye and I give the phone back to Uncle Lou.

"Well?" Carly says as Uncle Lou leaves the room.

"I'm so fired."

"Just let him try to fire you," Marilee says. Her eyes

blaze. "Your heart was in the right place so he shouldn't even try to make you feel bad."

"It's got nothing to do with my heart. I'm just trying to give the girls a fair deal."

"And you're absolutely right," Carly agrees. "It's perfectly normal for those girls to want to do some of the high-school things other girls get to do. They live on the street, not the moon. They see other kids going to these things. What does he expect?"

I look around at my friends. It feels good just knowing they're ready to jump up and defend me.

"Do you want us to go with you tomorrow? We can hang out with the girls while you talk to Mark." Marilee asks. "I wouldn't mind seeing Joy again anyway."

Joy was the homeless teenager who caused us to locate the shelter in the first place. She has spent some time at the Pews, and the Sisterhood all know her. When we first met Joy, she was so malnourished that we thought she had cancer, but she didn't and she's doing fine now.

I nod. "Thanks. I'd like that."

Seven years ago, I wouldn't have asked for any help. I thought I needed to do everything by myself. But—even if I haven't found a heart like the Tin Man wanted—I have learned a thing or two from being in the Sisterhood. One of them is that we're a whole lot stronger together than we are separately.

"We should take the journal, too," Carly adds.

The Sisterhood gave me our shared journal several months ago. It's just a regular school notebook, but it has pages of writing from when Marilee and Carly had it. I believe in taking my turn with things and it is my turn.

We all put our thoughts in the journal, but there's always one person who organizes it.

"I'm sorry," I say. "I keep forgetting to write in it. I know you all want to write your things, too."

"We're patient," Marilee says.

"You've just been waiting for the right time. I can understand that," Carly adds with a smile. "It can be a little intimidating."

I try not to bristle at that. "I'm not intimidated."

Really, I'm not. I don't like the way the others are looking at me though, so I do the only thing I can think of to distract everyone.

"I don't think Marilee finished all her praying," I say. "She said earlier she was going to pray for Rose. We can't forget Rose."

Fortunately, Marilee likes to pray these days and she's willing to turn the conversation in that direction. Marilee gives us a nice prayer about how much we all love Rose and, while we know she's helping other kids with cancer, we miss her at our meetings and want God to bless her.

I don't know what to say when we open our eyes so I just smile at the others.

I hate to admit it, but Marilee looks beautiful after she prays. I don't know what that's about, but I don't want to ask, either, so I bring the conversation back to the journal just to show I'm not afraid of it.

This journal was Marilee's idea. She wants a record of us taking back our lives after the cancer. She has some idea that it will help people who read it, and I don't disagree with that. She's already made plans to give copies of it to cancer-support groups, especially those that have teenage members. Maybe it'll even be a book.

But just because I think the journal is a good idea, it doesn't mean I need to like writing in it.

"Honestly, I don't know what to write," I say. "That's the only problem."

"You can start with a list of rules if you'd like," Marilee says to me.

"Well, rule number one is that you can't fire volunteers," I say and the others laugh a little even though it's not that funny. It's their way of supporting me.

Now, they're going to expect me to write something though, even if it is only rules.

I don't tell anyone that I have the journal stuck in my yarn bag. I've been carrying it back and forth to Sisterhood meetings for the past several months, just like I've been carrying that old ball of beige yarn. I couldn't seem to leave either one of them behind when I came to the Sisterhood meetings, but I haven't wanted to pull either one of them out, either.

I look at the beige yarn. It looks like overcooked oatmeal. At least I finally brought that into the light. I was tempted to leave it at the bottom of my knitting bag for the next hundred years. And now, I'm knitting it into a scarf. I'll donate it when I'm done; there's always someone who needs a bit of warmth in winter. That yarn will be useful even if it is ugly, so I'm making my peace with it.

I wish the same could be said for the journal.

If it was just a matter of organizing the others to write in the journal, I could do that. But the person who has the journal is supposed to do most of the writing and everyone knows how I feel about spilling my emotions out there for everyone to see. I'm not even sure what my emotions are. There's really no way to take over writing in the journal without letting my emotions come out.

I know we've made an agreement that we can fold back pages that we don't want the others to read, but I don't think anyone would like it if I folded all of my pages back.

I'm so jittery tonight that I dropped a stitch in that old yarn just before I put down my needles. I'll have to fix that before I go home. I'm a pretty good knitter by now, and I only drop stitches when I am nervous about something.

Fortunately, none of the other sisters ask me why I'm nervous tonight. I wouldn't know whether to say it was because of the meeting tomorrow with Mark or the journal sitting in the bottom of my yarn bag. Both of them have me a little tense.

While it is true that I never cried when I had the cancer (not even when no one could see me), I did start to show my stress back then because I would get the hiccups. They wouldn't be bad hiccups, but they'd come out of me like tiny drumbeats. I'd have to walk around to distract myself so they'd go away. I feel like I might need to hiccup right now.

I stand up just to give myself some room to move. It's almost time to leave anyway, so I decide to fix my dropped stitch when I get home. It's dark outside, but there are plenty of people walking along the sidewalks in Old Town Pasadena. The air is cool, and the urge to hiccup passes as I walk past the smoothie place. Then I turn the corner and go to the parking structure where I left my car.

I think about that dropped stitch I had tonight as I get into my car. We hadn't even learned to knit when we picked our name, The Sisterhood of the Dropped Stitches. Rose had pulled the four of us together into a group and, when we balked at forming a support group, she promised to teach us to knit while we talked. We didn't agree on much back then, but we all agreed on the name for our group. We each felt like we had dropped stitches inside of us. That something hadn't been knitted together correctly and that's why we had cancer.

Back then, Marilee blamed God for the dropped stitches in her body. Carly and Lizabett may have blamed Him, too, even if they weren't brave enough to say it. As for me, I knew better. I didn't blame God. I blamed myself. I didn't know which rule I had broken, but I knew it must have been a big one to give me cancer.

Chapter Two

"People do not wander around and then find themselves at the top of Mount Everest."
                                        —Zig Ziglar, motivational author

*I was the one who brought this quote to the Sisterhood
meeting. I kept trying to make my point that we needed
rules and a plan, long after everyone else had given up
on the subject. After a while I understood. It was hard to
focus on Mount Everest when we could barely get out of
bed and walk to the bathroom. Still, we had to have goals
and rules. They were our guide to survival. I was convinced of that. I hadn't discovered what rule I had broken
that gave me the cancer, but I was determined to find it.*

Okay, so I'm starting to write in the journal. I listen for
some big thunderclap from the night sky to mark the
event, but nothing happens so I keep going. This is Becca
by the way. I'm sitting at home, cross-legged on my bed
and trying to think of something to write in the journal.

It's easy for Marilee to say I should write down some rules, but when I sit here and try to do that, I can't think of any rules that seem important enough to put down. "Love your neighbor" is a good one, but that's nothing original. And the thing about flossing one's teeth every day is a rule everyone knows, so it's not worth putting down.

I stare at my walls for a minute hoping to get some inspiration. All that happens is that I notice the pink stripes in my wallpaper are looking even more yellowed. The paper's been on these walls a long time. I had planned to move out of my parents' house when I graduated from college, but now that I'm going to law school, I guess it will have to wait. I wonder if I should buy some new wallpaper. This one has little princesses here and there on it.

Until recently, I would not have considered changing the paper. My mother bought it for my room before I was even adopted, and I didn't want to change it, not after she'd gone to that kind of trouble. Even though I wasn't a princess-type of girl. Lately, though, I've decided the paper looks worn, so I tell myself there should be no offense in me wanting something new.

But I'm supposed to be thinking of rules and not my bedroom. Maybe I'll be able to think of some rules tomorrow after I meet with Mark. "Do not be mad at the volunteer" strikes me as a good rule, as well as, "Forgiveness is a girl's best friend."

In the meantime, I'm going to admit that I've started to wonder why rules are so important to me.

I'm not going to get all deep and emotional about it, but I do wonder. I vaguely remember when I first saw that wallpaper. I was six years old when I stepped into my new bedroom and realized my mother had expected a different kind of little girl. I was afraid my new mother would send me back to the foster home because I wasn't sweet enough. When she asked me if I liked the wallpaper, I assured her I did. At that time, I was desperate to stay and worried that my new mother would discover I didn't have a thing in common with those pink-skirted princesses.

Even back then, I was a Tin Man kind of a girl. The more nervous I got, the more I relied on my rules. The only thing anyone had ever told me about how to keep my new parents happy was that I was supposed to obey all of their rules. So I did everything right. I didn't even walk on the cracks of sidewalks just to be on the safe side. Or cry if I fell down.

Fortunately, my new parents seemed to like rules, too. My mother never said if she realized I wasn't the kind of little girl she'd dreamed of adopting. I used to hope she would tell me she knew the princess-look didn't fit me and that it was okay. But she never did. That convinced me she was a little disappointed in me.

I know both of my parents tried their best. Everything in our family back then was measured and as close to fair as it could be. Not that it was always easy to know what was fair since I had no sisters or brothers. My parents tried to measure me by other kids though. If the girl next door got a clown for her birthday party, I got one, too.

That's one of the reasons why my sickness was so traumatic for all of us. My mother in particular wanted me to have the same advantages as the other kids; that's the promise she told me she had made when she and my dad adopted me. But no one could control the cancer. It was unfair and there was nothing she could do about it. She couldn't even give me enough lollipops or pony rides to even it all out.

In high school, I missed all of the fun times.

When I was seventeen, the closest I got to prom night was watching the girl next door leave with her date in a white limo. I'd turned the lights out in my bedroom so Diane Stevens wouldn't see me sitting by my window watching her. I hadn't meant to watch, telling myself it was silly. But I did it anyway at the last minute. My mother must have known I would because she'd turned on our porch light so I'd see the couple better in the darkness.

After the girl and her date were gone, my mother brought me in a cup of cocoa. I couldn't drink more than a sip or two, but it made me feel better.

"She looked like a princess," I whispered, not even sure why that was important.

My mother didn't answer; she just kissed the top of my head and left. I thought she was crying, but I wasn't sure. She never cried around me.

That night, I promised myself that someday I'd get dressed up and go to a fancy event. Maybe it would be an opera or a Broadway play, but I'd wear an evening gown and step into a limo with a man in a tux and look beautiful. And I'd tell my mother all about it.

I'd forgotten that promise to myself until I saw the looks on the girls' faces earlier today. The funny thing was that, even after all these years, I still felt I'd been cheated because I'd never gone any place as elegant as

I'd pictured in my dreams. I've never been the princess my mother wanted, not even for that one night that most girls have.

Now, sitting in my bedroom, I look over at the window. When I was sick years ago with the chemo, I often asked my mother to come in after the lights were out and raise the blinds so I could see the stars during the night. I used to talk to the stars in the same way that Marilee talks to her God. I think I even told them I wanted to have an evening to make up for my missed prom.

It's strange to remember the thoughts that had gone through my head when I thought I might be dying.

Well, that's enough writing for tonight. I feel better just writing down some of my memories. Maybe it won't be so bad to be in charge of the journal. And it's not like I need to do all of the writing. The others will help. I'll have to take the notebook with me tomorrow and let them know that it's open season for journaling again.

I live closer to the shelter than anyone else in the Sisterhood, so we decided I would meet the rest of them at the Thai fish market down the street from the shelter on Melrose Avenue. Parking is hard to find on Melrose and the owner of the fish market lets the volunteers from the shelter park in his back lot. Today, I'm particularly grateful for his kindness. There's a big moving truck that is almost blocking the street in front of the shelter, and no street parking is available anywhere.

I sit in my car, waiting for the others to arrive. It's May and the morning weather is chilly, but I roll down my window anyway. The parking lot is asphalt and there are little bits of trash all around its edges. Every evening the owner of the fish market has someone pick up the litter, but there's always more thrown down before morning comes. I see gum wrappers and those plastic sleeves that go around donuts. Only the beer bottles are always gone. Someone picks those up for recycling.

Marilee drives her car into the lot and parks it beside me.

"I almost made a wrong turn back there," Marilee says as she gets out of the car. "I came in on Vermont."

Carly and Lizabett are also opening their car doors.

We all do the hug thing. I always feel good when we do that.

"I can't wait to see the place," Lizabett says. She's almost bouncing. "You've told us so much about it."

"It needs work," I say just so they don't expect too much. "It's due for a paint job, but I think Mark is waiting for some big donor check to come in."

"Ohhhh," Carly says.

I know what she's thinking. "He didn't tell *me* personally about it. I just heard because everyone knows."

"Well, still—when a man has problems, he needs someone to confide in and—voilà." Carly gestures to me. "You've got good ears."

"I'm sure he'll take that into consideration," I say with a grin as I start leading the way to the shelter.

The thing about the Sisterhood is that we've faced death together. Every other problem pales in comparison when we're together because of that memory, especially when it's a new morning and we're feeling good.

The double doors to the shelter are wide open and

some guys in beige uniforms are taking boxes into the building. Someone must be making a donation to the shelter and having it professionally moved here. It's not the usual thing. We're in Hollywood and there are some rich eccentrics around. I hope there's a new sofa in the truck. The one in the lounge is covered in a burnt orange vinyl, and it's not very comfortable. The girls have all been complaining about it.

The kids are just finishing up breakfast when we step into the lobby area of the shelter. We can't see the dining room from here, but in the distance, I can hear the clank of dishes being loaded into the bins for washing so I know what's happening. It smells as if they had eggs and bacon this morning.

Speaking of which, I enjoy the smell of bacon cooking even though I can never decide if I should eat it or not. I'm not technically Jewish, and, even if I were, my parents are not totally strict about the diet part, but I wonder if it would be disrespectful of me to eat pork since they don't. I keep thinking someone will eventually tell me that it's okay for me to eat pork. Until then, I don't even eat turkey bacon just so I don't look like I wish I was allowed to break the rules. Breaking that rule would set me apart from my parents and I'm not sure I'm ready to do that without their blessing even at my age.

I can see into the back office area and it looks like Mark is already at work. He's standing in the doorway of his office talking to some of the movers.

"Let me go introduce you to the night crew," I say as I turn the Sisterhood in another direction and lead them into the dining room. There's no point in interrupting

Mark; I'll see him soon enough. "Joy should be around here somewhere."

We hear Joy's laugh before we even enter the room. The night supervisor sees us and comes over. I introduce everybody and head back out of the room.

I'm not in a hurry to talk to Mark, but I do want to get it over with before all of the kids start coming down the hall on their way to the computer lab. For some of the kids, their e-mail address is their only stable address, and they're always anxious to check for messages. The staff here monitor the e-mail messages to be sure no one is misusing the account to talk with a drug dealer or someone worse. Most kids though have long-term accounts and hope to hear from old friends.

I don't see the movers, but the door into Mark's office is open so I knock on the door frame.

"Becca?" Mark says as he looks up from the boxes that are open at his feet.

I relax the minute I see him. He doesn't look overwhelmingly angry or anything. He does look a little tired though. His hair isn't as combed as it usually is.

"Come in," he says as he gestures to the chair beside his desk. "If you can make it through all of these boxes."

He sits down at his desk, and I sit in the chair.

I was in Mark's office when I first interviewed to volunteer at the shelter, but it didn't look like it does today. "New desk?"

"Don't ask," he says.

The desk in front of us looks like it's made of solid walnut. With a high polish, it's one of those things that tells you the owner has money and isn't afraid to spend it.

"Well, it looks great."

"It's yours if you want it. I was doing just fine with the computer cart."

I see the computer cart is pushed into the far corner of his office now. It's scratched up and one of the wheels is missing. I think I see a wad of duct tape on one of the legs. The cart looks like it's made out of particleboard.

"I don't need a desk," I say.

"Neither do I. But try telling that to my grandmother. I don't need all of my law books, either. Or the office chair she's sending to go with the desk. Solid walnut. Do you know how hard walnut wood is?"

I shake my head.

Mark keeps looking at me. "I don't suppose you have a grandmother?"

I shake my head again.

"Well, grandmothers have a way of only wanting what's best for you," Mark says and his lips turn up in a smile. "The problem is that they're convinced they know what that best thing for you is, even if you don't see it that way."

"I always thought having a grandmother would be nice." I don't really see the problem in giving up that computer cart for the desk and chair his grandmother is sending, either.

"Well, at least she had sense enough to give up on finding me a girlfriend."

That is the first time I know for sure that Mark isn't dating anyone seriously. The girls at the shelter, of course, keep saying he isn't, but they say it in a way that is half

asking me if I know anything more than they do on the subject. I pretend I'm not interested, but secretly I'd been wondering, too.

I think of what Carly says about my ears that are good for listening. Somehow it doesn't seem like enough to just sit here and listen to his problems. I try to show empathy. "Well, that must be—ah—good."

"Anyway, I think she's given up." Mark stops to frown and stares off into space. "I can never be sure with my grandmother."

Just then the movers come to the door with another load of boxes.

"She must care about you."

Mark grunts, but his attention has moved to the boxes. "Just put them in the corner."

"I can come back later today," I say.

"No, wait." Mark turns his attention back to me. "I need to apologize to you and I'd like to do it now. I shouldn't have been so sharp with you last night."

I take a quick breath. I'm willing to meet him halfway. "I know I was out of line telling the girls anything without checking and—"

"No." Mark holds up his hand to stop me. "There's no point in having a woman like you around for the girls to talk to, if I don't listen to what you say."

"Really?"

He nods. "I've decided that, if you think the girls need some kind of a prom, we'll try to pull it off."

I'm so surprised I don't know what to say.

"How we're going to do it though I have no idea. A prom would be—" He trails off and shakes his head.

I kind of like it when he looks bewildered.

"I told them a prom or something like it," I say. "They really only want the fun of dressing up and having something formal to go to. It'll be good for them, too. They'll learn how to act in that kind of setting."

Mark nods. "I'm fine with all that. It's just that everything we do is group-focused. I'm trying to build teams with the kids. A prom is always a date thing."

"We can do a banquet," I say. "No one needs a date to eat."

"But we eat all the time. Will that be enough?"

"If they can dress up like it's the prom and go there in a limo, then—yes, I think they'll be quite happy. A prom is about the glamour of it all."

"We'd still have to raise extra money," Mark says, but I can see he is thinking about the idea. "You're welcome to talk to my grandmother. She's involved in lots of charities and knows all about donating money. Besides, it'll give her something to think about besides me."

"Oh, I—"

"Not that you won't have to do some work to convince her," Mark says. "She doesn't like to give to unauthorized programs."

"We'd be unauthorized?"

"Beyond the scope of the annual plan that was approved by the board," Mark says as he shrugs.

"Well, I— I'm speechless. I'm not suggesting anything radical."

"Of course not, but my grandmother will think it's foolish to stray from the annual plan that the board approved. She's just that way."

"There's nothing wrong with a plan." Ordinarily, I'd agree with his grandmother.

I can see Mark is still thinking about everything. "We need to be sure the kids all know this thing is tame. I want to be sure everybody is onboard with the expectations. I don't want the girls expecting more than we're giving them."

Mark looks me squarely in the eyes.

"I'll go in right now and ask them if a conservative formal banquet would be enough to make them happy. Nothing radical."

"Make sure you say there'll be no dates. And no dancing."

"Got it," I say as I stand up to leave. Then I hesitate. "But the guys will be there, won't they? I'm not sure I could talk the girls into an all-female banquet. Even if no one is paired off, the girls will want, you know—someone to see how good they look. It can't be that tame that it's only girls."

"Oh, the guys will be there," Mark says grimly. "Maybe something like this will make them finally pull together as a team."

"It'll be good for them," I say with a smile now that I know we're moving ahead. "It'll help them understand women, too."

Mark grunts. "I've been to dozens of those kinds of things and I don't have a clue about women. I can't even figure out my *grandmother*. The guys will probably be about the same."

Now I'm really smiling. I don't suppose I should be happy that Mark Russo doesn't think he knows anything about women, but I am. It's nice to find a guy who isn't so full of himself. Besides, I'm glad I can be a little mysterious on behalf of women everywhere.

I don't even have time for the warmth of it all to reach my heart, before Mark continues.

"I wish more women were like you," he says suddenly.

Okay, so—that sounds a little good, but there's something missing in the tone of his voice.

"You've got a good head on your shoulders," he adds.

"Oh."

Even though it should be a compliment, I leave Mark's office knowing it's not the compliment I want. Something about the way Mark said those words while his attention was really on the boxes the men behind us were moving around makes me wonder if he even sees me as a woman. Maybe he only likes women who want to be princesses, too. Not that it matters. I don't have time for a romance or anything. Still, I would like him to think I'm at least as mysterious as his *grandmother.*

I only get halfway down the hall before I see that the girls are clustered in the main lounge.

"Well?" Lupe asks. Even with her missing tooth, she's the least shy of all the girls. "What'd he say?"

"He said we could start talking about it," I say. "And, then—if we all understand what we're agreeing to do— we can have something."

"With cool dresses?" Lupe asks.

"And limos?" Candice asks.

"Here's the deal," I say as I motion for them all to sit down. I join them on the carpeted floor. "We can have a formal event that is like a prom, but not a prom. No pairing off and dancing, but maybe a banquet."

"Would there be food at the banquet?"

I smile. I should have thought of this. All of these kids like food. I mean really like it. I'm sure it comes from having been hungry so often in their lives. "There will be lots of food and it will be awesome."

"A banquet's good," Lupe says and the others nod in agreement.

"As long as we get those dresses, too," Candice adds. She's a black girl from the south and, even with the scar on her cheek, she's tall and elegant. "And some high heels. None of these squared-off things that are good for your feet. I want the pointy ones."

The girls and I spend the next few minutes planning what they're going to wear. Of course, none of them have anything but T-shirts and jeans right now. But I figure there's no reason to have a dream unless you're willing to reach up to grab it and high heels will only help with that.

Chapter Three

"I don't think anyone should write their autobiography until after they're dead."

—Samuel Goldwyn

Lizabett surprised us with this quote in one Sisterhood meeting. On some of her most discouraging days, she wanted to laugh. We all did. I'm convinced there's only so much distress any of us can take and then we need to laugh. We spent our meeting that night sketching out our autobiographies and deciding which actress we wanted to play us if our autobiographies were ever made into movies. I chose Julia Roberts to play me, telling the others that at least I would have heart when I was dead then. I joked that she could play me better than I could play myself.

After we finished that night, I wondered if the reason Rose kept a copy of what we each had written was because she wanted to have something to read at our funerals. I surprised myself because I didn't really mind

*so much. Especially if she mentioned how hard I had tried
to do all the right things so I would live. It wasn't dying
that bothered me in the end; it was the defeat of it that I
couldn't abide. I felt like I would be a failure if I let the
cancer take me, and that I could not tolerate.*

Hi, this is Becca again. The Sisterhood is sitting in the
lounge with some of the girls from the shelter, and we're
making a list of what we need to pull off a banquet. So
far we've noted that we need a place to hold the event,
some tablecloths, food, a selection of evening gowns,
new shoes, tuxedoes for the men (those can be rented),
ten stretch limos and, well, more shoes. Several of the
girls say they're willing to wear an old sheet wrapped
around them if they have to, but they want killer shoes.

"And, those little finger bowls," Candice adds. "I saw
them in a movie once. They're just too cool. You dip
your little fingers in them and, la-dee-dah, it's like you're
dining with the Queen."

I write down finger bowls on the list all the while
wondering how Candice nurtured a secret desire for
finger bowls in her life. She ran away from an abusive
home when she was eleven. I can guarantee there were
no finger bowls in that house.

Except for her scar, Candice looks like an ordinary
fifteen-year-old now, but I know she's spent the past four
years on the streets. She refused to go into the foster-care
system, so she had to know how to run fast and hide from
the police. She says she got her scar in a fight with her
drunken father the night she left home and she hasn't
been inclined to trust adults since. At first, I thought she'd

be reserved around me, but I guess I'm still young enough that she doesn't see me as an adult.

All Candice is focused on now is finger bowls and high heels, though.

I don't know how we are going to get everything we need. Especially the place. It would be perfect to have it at the ballroom of the Ritz-Carlton hotel down Oak Knoll Avenue. They have this beautiful driveway lit by hundreds of white lights and doormen in uniform who would look so cool opening the limo doors when we arrive, but I'm sure it would cost way too much to rent the ballroom. Most of the big hotels around Los Angeles have ballrooms that we can't afford, either.

If we can't find any place to rent, Marilee has offered up the Pews, assuming we'd schedule our banquet for Monday night when the diner is usually closed. So we have a Plan B on the location. We're going to look for a rental hall first though. There is also a country club on Altadena Drive that might be a possibility. We'll need to find out what they charge.

Carly has said she'll put the word out with the people she knows in San Marino that she's looking for used formal gowns. She doesn't know how many she'll get, but the people there do go to black-tie events all the time. We have no Plan B for dresses so I hope Carly is persuasive. She's also going to ask about shoes.

The girls are excited just talking about the clothes. Lupe decides she wants a red dress with a swooping back. Or, she tells me, maybe a flame orange color would do. I ask her if she'll settle for yellow and she's still thinking about that. In the end, most of the gowns we get will probably be old bridesmaid dresses so a yellow dress is more likely to show up than a red or an orange one.

Lizabett offers to ask her three firefighter brothers to help set up tables and everything. And, she said their friends might help us, too.

But the limos? That's what stops us in our planning. Where will we get the money for the limos? None of us even know how much that would cost. Marilee offers to do some calling later and find out how expensive it would be for limo rides.

I decide we need to take a break. It's time for the girls to go to their GED class anyway. I'm going to give the journal to Marilee. I want to think without a pen in my hand for a minute. That's how I think best. And, a good brain is nothing to be ashamed of, I tell myself, thinking back to Mark's comment. Where would men be if women didn't have good brains?

I don't know why Becca gave me the journal, but I'm going to write in it for a few minutes anyway. This is Marilee. I haven't seen Becca this stressed since before she got her acceptance letter for law school. That was supposed to be her last big hurdle for a while. She's supposed to be relaxing now, especially because she's on vacation from her internship with the judge.

But I hear a tiny little hiccup as she sits here, and I know what that means.

It's because of Mark, of course. I knew when Becca first told me that he'd earned his law degree and then given it up to work in the shelter that he would be an irresistible puzzle to her. Becca is not used to people who win the race and then don't march right up to collect the trophy.

He's clearly committed to this place and these kids. He walked over here while we were making our list and he talked with each of the girls for just a little bit. They each beamed when they had his attention.

This place is really helping these girls. Well, and the boys, too. Becca has said Mark worries that the kids don't see themselves as a team yet, but we can hear laughter from various parts of the building. And the kids all look clean and well-fed. There are bowls of fruit sitting around the lounge and one of the kids was vacuuming in here a few minutes ago. I think the kids here are doing well.

The shelter smells like a home instead of an institution and I think that says volumes for the place. The carpet is a deep blue instead of that moss green I've noticed in so many older public buildings. And the furniture, while mismatched, is the kind found in a living room instead of a doctor's office.

Of course, the shelter works with the child-welfare authorities, especially with the younger children who come here, but it doesn't feel bureaucratic.

I'm going to stop writing pretty soon. It sounds as if Becca is ready for all of us to go back to Pasadena. The movers are just bringing a wooden desk chair into the building though, so we sit and watch that. This is the second trip for the movers, and Mark is looking more and more harried.

Mark tells the movers to put the desk chair out in the lounge area. They obviously don't like the idea, but they do it anyway. Becca told us about Mark's grandmother and

I'm looking forward to hearing how Becca's meeting with the older woman goes. Mark already told Becca she should make an in-person appointment to meet with his grandmother instead of asking her for any help over the phone.

Becca is a force to be reckoned with, but it sounds like Mark's grandmother is, too.

There. It's time to wrap this up for now. I'll give the journal back to Becca. I didn't read what she's already written, but I'm glad she's started to write. Even if she's just copying recipes, it will get her going.

This is Becca again. Marilee, if you ever do read this, I want you to know I have better things to do than copy recipes. I don't even cook.

Although, maybe that will change now that we're starting to plan the banquet. Someone needs to cook for it, especially if we rent a hall or something like that. Candice wants us to have chicken cordon bleu. She saw it on a cooking show. For a girl who spent the past four years on the street, she sure has watched a lot of movies and television. I suppose though that the movies make sense. It would be warm and dry in the theatre, and I suspect she has a way of sneaking inside. And she could watch television at the department stores. Again, it would be warm and dry.

I don't think I've ever watched a cooking show in my life. I did watch a trial once between two chefs who co-owned a restaurant and were taking each other to court for misusing funds. It turns out they didn't agree on the recipes they wanted to use, either.

I'm sitting on my bed at home writing in the journal, but when I finish here I'm going to go to the kitchen and take down my mother's *Joy of Cooking* recipe book from its shelf. My mother has always said that particular cookbook can tell a person how to make anything they want. It must have a recipe for chicken cordon bleu.

I know it would be easier to just buy some kind of a frozen chicken dish, but I want the kids to feel special at this banquet. No one feels that way if they're served a piece of chicken from a freezer box.

Speaking of feeling better, when I'm out in the kitchen, I'll make myself a cup of cocoa. That always makes me feel better.

I turn on the light over the stove in the kitchen instead of using the main overhead light. It's after ten o'clock, and I don't want to wake up my parents. I'm quiet as I pull the cookbook off the shelf and carry it over to the table, but I've barely sat down when my mother comes into the kitchen.

"Feeling okay?" she asks. My mother is fifty-seven years old. She's got dark hair and small bones. I sometimes wonder if she picked my picture out of the adoption books because I looked like her.

I nod. The okay question stopped being casual when I was diagnosed years ago, and my mother still asks it like she's afraid to hear my answer.

"I'm just looking up a recipe for chicken cordon bleu," I add. "For the prom banquet."

That's what I've started calling our event—a prom banquet. We might not have any dancing, but we'll hopefully have live music. Lizabett is working on that. And it will be nice.

I'd already briefed my mother on the prom banquet earlier this evening. I didn't mention the food part though. Or the fancy dresses. I don't know how she'll feel about me arranging for these girls to go to a prom event when she's never been able to help me dress up for something like that. I have a feeling that would have been an important thing for my mother and me. She would have had one of those moments she'd hoped for when she adopted me.

"I shouldn't have thrown away those big glass baking pans. You remember the ones," my mother says as she yawns and pulls her white terry-cloth robe closer around her. "You could bake for an army with them."

"They would have worked good."

My mother has a strict policy of giving away or throwing away anything that she hasn't used recently. No one ever has anything old in the Snyder household. There's not a cracked dish anywhere and all of the pictures on the walls are rotated monthly. I don't know why she does that last bit. I'm not sure she even knows since she can never give me a reason other than that her mother used to do the same thing.

"Want some cocoa?" I mark the page in the cookbook where it talks about ways to cook chicken and push my chair back from the table. "I'm just getting ready to put some water on to heat."

My mother nods and sits down at the table. "It's nice to see you have time to relax in the evening now that you've got some free time with your internship."

I walk over to the stove. "That internship is helping me get into law school. I'm glad to have it."

"I know," my mother says.

Sometimes I wonder if my parents understand the importance of what I am doing. I have taken all of the right steps so that I would get accepted into a good law school. "Not everybody gets accepted, you know."

My mother shrugs. "You would have found a way even without the internship."

I take a deep breath and let it go. I can't expect my mother to know how competitive it is out there. She just expects me to come through on things. She has no idea that I hang out there by my teeth most of the time. I have to work for my successes. No one has ever handed me any victory.

When the water is hot, I stir in the cocoa mix and take two cups to the table. We sit and talk for a while. I tell my mother again all about the law school, and she listens. I think she's a little proud. I hope so, at least. Sometimes it's hard for me to read other people.

I have a message on my cell phone the next morning when I get up. It is Carly, and she wants me to have lunch with the Sisterhood today. The Sisterhood doesn't usually get together for lunch on a Saturday, but I'm happy to meet. I'll start back into my internship in a couple of weeks, and I'll miss most of the casual lunch meetings. Now that Carly and Marilee both work at the Pews, it's easy for them to have lunch together. Lizabett is there often, too, because she's taking summer school classes at Pasadena City College.

I'm the only one who usually can't do lunch.

All of a sudden, that fact stands out for me in blinding clarity. I should write in the journal about that when I get a chance. I hadn't quite realized that I'm always the odd

person out in anything that we do as the Sisterhood. I'm the one who asks the hard questions. I'm the one who takes the unpopular stand. I'm the one who can never do lunch.

It's me who is always out of step with the others. Even when we all were so sick, I was the one who insisted we needed to carry on our lives. I wonder how the others feel about that. Then I wonder if I'm missing something by not blending in better. Do I always have to be the one who doesn't really fit in?

Sometimes I'm lonely and I wonder if this is why. Maybe I should try to just blend in better. Even as I think it, I realize I won't be able to do it. Maybe I'm just destined to be the one who's not in step. Maybe I even want it that way.

It takes me a beat or two before I wonder if it has something to do with me being adopted. Maybe I don't feel I deserve to belong anywhere.

I sit still on my bed and let those thoughts sink in. I don't think I'll write about this in the journal, after all. Instead, I get dressed. I put on a white blouse and jeans. At least, in clothes like these, I will look like I blend in anywhere in Los Angeles.

Chapter Four

"If one morning I walked on top of the water across the Potomac River, the headline that afternoon would read 'President Can't Swim'."

—Lyndon B. Johnson, on his
relationship with reporters

I have often felt like people don't quite understand me. This is Becca and I brought this quote to one of the later Sisterhood meetings. The odd thing was that everyone seemed to actually understand me better when I was sick than when I became healthy. I wondered if people just put more effort into listening to me when they were worried about me. I asked the others in the Sisterhood, and, after they thought about it a minute, they agreed they, too, seemed to have been better understood when they had cancer. I felt like I had discovered some great thing about how to get along with people. Of course, I would rather be misunder-

*stood than sick so the realization did me little good
other than to give me some sympathy for people who
pretend to be sick.*

I am sitting down in the room at the Pews where the Sisterhood usually meets. This is Becca and I drove here instead of taking the bus, so I'm a little earlier than I thought I would be. I don't mind. It's giving me some time to write in the journal.

I am hoping that, when the people who Marilee thinks will read this journal actually do read this journal, they will understand me just like people seemed to when I was sick. It's a comforting thought. When we read something someone wrote about themselves, I think we actually understand the person better than if they were to tell us about it themselves in casual conversation.

Everything is just more concrete in black and white.

Anyway, I think I'm going to take a picture of this room and stick it in the journal. This room shows our journey. There are French doors that connect it to the main dining room at the Pews. The panes in those doors are the only windows in the room so it is always a little dark in here. I've often thought it makes our room seem a little like a cave. A warm and friendly cave, protected from everything. It was just what we needed in the beginning. I remember thinking I could so totally understand an animal crawling away to their cave when they knew they were going to die.

For a while, this room was our cave. And, then, as we started to heal, we added things to the room, like Lizabett's calendar of France. The calendar is several years old now, but we still leave it hanging on the wall because one of Lizabett's goals is to visit France, and she hasn't gone there yet. She wants to see Monet's garden. She used to talk about him painting water when all of the other painters just looked through it. The calendar with its water lilies is her first step in planning that trip, and I always feel good when I see it. She's still saving money to go. Some day she'll make the trip.

There are several books in the case behind the table that tell about the nativity. They're there because Carly played Mary in a nativity performance last Christmas. And, of course, we have a couple of books about knitting just in case one of us wants to try a more complicated pattern. Rose gave us those through the years.

I love this room. It feels more like home to me than my room in my parents' house. For one thing, I don't have to pretend to like the wallpaper. The Sisterhood pretty much knows me and accepts me. I am who I am here, and it feels good. They accept that I'm more like the prime minister than the royal princess. They would never hang frilly pink creatures on my walls and expect me to feel at home.

Yes, I'm definitely going to take a picture of this place. No one has taken a picture for the journal yet, so I hope I get Sisterhood points for being creative. At least, everyone should agree that I'm giving this journal some thought.

Ah, I think I hear Carly. She works at the Pews waiting tables now while she's taking more college classes. I know she's just dying to write some in this journal, so I might leave it with her while I go make my call to Mark's grandmother. I'd called her phone number earlier today, but I didn't get an answer. I want to set up an appointment as soon as possible.

This is Carly and Becca is right. I have been wanting to write in the journal. I feel like it's connecting with an old friend when I hold the notebook in my hand. This journal got me through some rough patches with my family, and I want to record that things are going well for all of us. My mother moved out of my uncle's house (he was supporting us while my dad was in rehab for his alcohol problem), and she has moved in with my father in his small apartment in Eagle Rock, just next to Pasadena. I think they're happier together now than I ever remember seeing them.

I'm renting an efficiency apartment above some stores on the corner of Hill and Washington in the northern part of Pasadena. With the money I make waiting tables at the Pews three nights a week, I am able to support myself, and it feels good. I still have plenty of time for classes and to spend with my boyfriend, Randy Parker. He was Marilee's fantasy boyfriend all the time she had breast cancer, but, once she was well, it turned out she really liked Lizabett's brother, Quinn Macdonald, better.

And I'm glad she did, because I like Randy a lot. He and I both attend the same church Marilee goes to and my life has never been better. I'm feeling good about myself, my parents and my God.

I still get goose bumps when I realize I can actually pray to the God of the universe, and He listens. Wow. And my parents are finally talking to me like I'm an adult. And then there's Randy.

I wish I could give some of my good feelings to Becca. I'd willingly share. Becca still doesn't look relaxed in her life. I pray sometimes that she will find what she is looking for. I keep hoping that working with the kids at the shelter will help her find what she needs. I've often wondered if she doesn't need to talk more about how it was for her to be adopted.

Of course, I didn't talk about my problems for a long time, so I'm hardly an example to follow. But Becca has always seemed so upfront about everything else.

I know lots of kids are adopted as babies, so they probably don't have any memories of those years without parents. But Becca was older; I think she was six or so. That's old enough to have some definite impressions of what life was like. I mean, did she have enough to eat? Was she ever afraid? Did anyone sing her lullabies when she couldn't go to sleep? And then there's the big question. Is she angry with her natural mother for giving her up? I keep expecting her to talk about those things with us, but she never does. She doesn't even know who her real mother is, and that would depress me. I may not always be happy with my parents, but at least they're my for-sure parents and I know them. They didn't leave me behind when things got tough.

I'm hoping that working with these girls at the shelter will help Becca. Most of those girls have been betrayed in some way by their parents, too.

Speaking of the shelter, I haven't told Becca yet, but I've located two formal evening gowns. They belong to my aunt, but I think that with a couple of tucks and some new hems they will work fine for two of the girls. I know we have quite a few more dresses to locate, but I've got my aunt on the job, as well. She knows a lot of women in San Marino, so we'll see.

Shoes are going to be the big problem. No one seems to want to give any shoes away. And a dress can be altered, but shoes have to be the right size. And all of the girls want special shoes. It must be the Cinderella fantasy. They all think the guys are going to be looking at their shoes.

Ah, here comes Becca back. Lizabett is with her, and Marilee is just stepping out of the kitchen.

"I did it," Becca announces the minute she opens the French doors. "I'm all set up to see Mrs. Russo at her place tomorrow morning at seven o'clock."

"Sunday morning?" Marilee asks as she follows Becca into the room.

Becca shrugs as she pulls a chair out from the table. "She picked the time."

"She probably thinks you won't show up." Marilee says as she finds her place at the table. "Incidentally, I put our order in."

We all have a usual order when we come to the Pews and Marilee had asked us earlier if anyone wanted to make any changes for today. We didn't; we like our usual.

"Mrs. Russo doesn't know our Becca." Lizabett says with satisfaction. She's the last one to sit down at the table. "Becca would be there at six o'clock if she needed to be."

Well, I (Carly) need to sign off. I'm going to hand this journal over to Becca. I'm sure she'll want to tell you all about her meeting with Mrs. Russo. I plan to get up early tomorrow morning so I can pray. Becca might not know it, but I have a feeling she's going to need some help with the older woman.

This is Becca. I glanced at the last lines Carly wrote when she handed the journal back to me at the table.

"I can handle it," I look up from the journal and say to everyone. "No one needs to make a big deal out of it. She's a *grandmother*. How difficult can she be?"

"You don't have a grandmother, do you?" Marilee asks.

I shake my head, even though I don't know for sure. Maybe I technically did have a grandmother before I was adopted. Maybe I still do, for that matter, even if I've never heard of her.

"They can be formidable."

"I always wanted a grandmother," Lizabett adds to what Marilee has said. "One who bakes cookies."

"I don't think Mrs. Russo bakes cookies," Carly says and then turns to me. "What did she say her address was anyway?"

"It's a block west on Huntington Drive if you come down San Gabriel. Five, eight something. I wrote it down."

Carly nods her head. "I thought so. She's in the heart of San Marino. Maybe you want to stay with me tonight so you don't have to drive in from North Hollywood."

I'm the only one of the Sisterhood who doesn't live around Pasadena. Not that I'm that far away, but it would be nice to save the half-hour drive in the morning on the 101 freeway. "Thanks, I'll do that."

"Good." Carly nods. "We can stay up tonight and make one of your lists of what you want to say to her."

Marilee and I are both noted for our list-making skills.

"I just plan to explain to her that life hasn't been fair for these girls and that she can do something to make it right. People like to make a difference."

Carly nods. "That's a place to start."

"You don't think she'll see the reason of that?" I hadn't really expected to need to go further. "She sounds like a rational person."

"People are seldom rational when you're asking for their money," Carly says. "You need to touch their hearts."

"I can do that," I say, trying not to be defensive. "Just because I don't get all emotional all the time, that doesn't mean I can't—you know."

Marilee nods. "You'll do fine."

"I would give to the cause if I had any extra money," Lizabett says. "Who wouldn't want girls to have an experience like that? And if we do a prom-like banquet—they are practically an institution in this country. I'm sure Mark's grandmother went to one when she was young."

"She might not have had banquets and proms when she was in school," Carly cautions. "But I'm sure Becca can tell her how important they are to girls today."

"Just be sure and say something nice about her dog," Marilee says as she looks at me. "Every older woman I've seen in San Marino has a little dog."

"I can do that."

"You should compliment her a lot about everything," Lizabett adds with a nod. "Especially tell her you like whatever food she's cooked for you."

"I don't think she's going to feed me."

"She's a grandmother. She won't be able to help herself," Lizabett says. "They all think young people are too skinny. She'll at least give you buttered toast."

"And don't say anything if she has her hair in those funny rubber curlers," Marilee adds. "Just pretend everyone wears them."

"Really, I'll be fine," I say even though I'm beginning to wonder by now.

"We're making a list tonight just in case," Carly says. "And I'm getting up with you in the morning to make you coffee before you leave to go see her."

"Don't let her eat anything," Lizabett says to Carly. "We want Becca to be hungry when she gets to the grand-mother's place. Grandmothers can tell if someone is just picking at their food, even if it is only toast."

I see one of the waitresses coming toward the French doors with a tray of salads. Our lunch has arrived. I smile at everyone as I close the journal. I haven't even had a chance to write anything. I take a deep breath. "Okay. I need coffee. No food. Dog compliments. I think I have it all. Don't worry."

"And write in the journal," Lizabett says. "That way we'll remember it forever and ever."

Now that's a scary thought. I put it out of my mind so that I can eat my Chinese chicken salad in peace, but I think about it later when I'm lying on Carly's sofa bed. She'd got an efficiency apartment so she's on a Murphy bed that comes out of the wall to my left.

She has two windows in her place, but the blinds are drawn so none of the night light comes inside. I can still see the outline of Carly lying on the Murphy bed though.

"Do you really think we should keep this journal going?" I ask softly. We only said our last good night five minutes ago so I don't think she's asleep yet.

"Marilee will kill us if we stop," Carly says, her voice drowsy.

"But to have our thoughts out there set in stone forever—that's a little, well, strange, isn't it?"

"People do it all the time."

"We don't," I say even though it's mostly me who doesn't now that Carly's started talking more about her problems.

Carly doesn't say anything to that and I let her go to sleep. I don't think she's as bothered by the shelf life of our thoughts as I am. But it unnerves me to realize people could be reading this journal when we're all dead. To me that's a little creepy. Maybe if Marilee ever does find someone to publish the journal, we can ask them to use some kind of paper that disintegrates after ten years or so. That should be long enough for our journal to last. I'm going to add a note to my list for tomorrow to talk to Marilee.

In the meantime, this bed is pretty comfortable. Carly washed the sheets with some kind of lavender stuff and the scent smells really good as I burrow my nose down into them. It's hard to remember that I have any problems when I lie here surrounded by lavender.

I think of Mark and that desk of his as I drift off to sleep. I wonder if he'll decide to keep the desk in his office or if I'll find it in the lounge when I go to the shelter next. I wonder if anyone would notice if I put a lavender candle on the desk if it's in the lounge. I wouldn't do it if the desk was in his office, of course. But the girls would like a lavender candle in the lounge.

Lavender smells like a spring evening.

Chapter Five

"I loathe people who keep dogs. They are cowards who haven't got the guts to bite people themselves."
—August Strindberg in "A Madman's Diary," 1895

Rose brought us this quote after we had been complaining about all of the shots we'd been getting when we were sick. Between the shots and the blood draws, our arms were filled with tiny little pinholes. Rose made the connection between needles and dog bites and, before we knew it, we shared an inside joke. If we saw each other in the hospital lab, we would ask each other how our dog bites were doing. Then we'd giggle and giggle. The staff probably thought we were half-crazy, but we didn't mind. I don't know how Rose knew a few shared jokes would help us become friends.

I'm thinking of that dog-bite quote as I look into Mrs. Russo's house. She has a maid who answers the door. At least, I assume the woman is the maid since she's wearing a white apron over a dark brown dress. Whoever she is, she's obviously here to do the dirty work of stopping any undesirables who want to get into the house so that Mrs. Russo doesn't have to. I can tell by the frown on the maid's face, that the current undesirable must be me.

"Mrs. Russo asked me to come," I say as the maid looks at me skeptically. "I'm Becca Snyder, from the shelter."

"Oh, you're from the shelter!" the maid says as her stern look vanishes, and she lights up with a smile. "Quick. Come with me. Mrs. Russo will want to know."

I'm glad I know the secret word to enter the kingdom. I barely have time to look around me as we walk through the entry and step into a very large room with a black marble floor. I can hear the clicks of my shoes as we continue through the room. The walls are white, and the whole room feels cool. Some filtered light comes through the white net curtains covering the sliding glass doors that line one wall. Three black leather couches are grouped together in the middle of the room with a round coffee table in the middle of them.

I'm surprised a grandmother would go for black leather instead of doilies, but I'm walking too fast to give it more than a passing thought. I have an index card in the pocket of my skirt and it has my list of items to remember. I hold on to it as we walk through the first room and come to a doorway leading to a second room.

The maid stops outside the room. "Mrs. Russo?"

I see an older woman inside, sitting at an office desk that could be a twin to the one that was delivered to Mark's office. The chair sitting beside it matches the chair that was delivered to him, too. I would think Mark had asked the movers to return the desk and the chair, except these have a settled look about them. There's a black device sitting on top of the desk and I hear garbled words coming through it. It looks like an old radio, but it must not be working right because Mrs. Russo is squinting at a page of what looks like directions and she's scowling.

Mark's grandmother is sitting military straight in her chair, and she doesn't have a bit of the soft grandmotherly look that Lizabett imagined. I don't think I'll get any buttered toast. Right now, I'm not even sure I'll get her attention.

Then she looks up at the maid. "What?"

"Someone is here from the shelter," the maid says like she's delivering good news.

Mrs. Russo blinks. "Oh, of course."

She'd clearly forgotten, but I'm not going to let that stop me.

"Mrs. Russo," I say. My index card tells me to step forward and offer to shake her hand, but I'm not sure that would be welcome so I just try to smile in a friendly way. I'm glad Carly insisted I borrow one of her skirts to wear. Nothing about Mrs. Russo is casual. "I'm so glad you agreed to meet with me when I called you yesterday."

I stop to give her time to remember.

"Do you know how to adjust this thing?" Mrs. Russo says as she ignores all of my cues and looks back at the old radio on her desk. "It says something about action bands and a warning system. My handyman had it working, but something's wrong now."

I tell myself Mrs. Russo must have been expecting me when she was getting dressed even if she then forgot she was having company. She is wearing a cream-colored silk dress that no one would put on just to sit at home and listen to the radio. Her white hair is cut short and stylish. She's wearing a light rose lipstick, and a pair of reading glasses hang from a gold chain around her neck. I don't see one dog hair on her cream dress so I figure some stereotypes are not true.

"I'm afraid I don't know anything about old radios." I smile to show I would help if I could. It seems a little sad that she doesn't have a little puffy dog that she cuddles.

Mrs. Russo finally takes a good look at me. "It's not a radio. It's a police scanner."

Okay, so now I'm not so worried about the little dog. I wonder if she has a pit bull she lets run around the yard instead. "I'm sure you don't need to worry too much about your security here. San Marino is generally very safe."

"I'm not worried for me. I got this so I can follow what's happening at the shelter. You know Mark is working nights now?"

This is definitely two strikes against me. She glares at me like I have something to do with the hours Mark works.

"I did hear that he's there nights," I say. "But I think it's only temporary."

"It's not safe at night. Half of those boys carry knives."

"Not in the shelter. There are rules against that."

Mrs. Russo snorts. "Those aren't the kind of boys who obey the rules."

What can I say? I know she's right. And, not all of the kids at the shelter are there because they've decided they want to live a peaceful life. "Still, there are procedures. Everyone is checked very thoroughly."

"There was a brawl of some sort last night just a block away from the shelter," she says. She lifts her hand to push back her hair and, all of a sudden, she looks frail. "You're right in the middle of gang territory there. It's just not safe. Even if everyone inside is unarmed, there are others outside just waiting."

She pauses and her shoulders slump.

"I don't think Mark would like you to worry," I say softly. I guess she is like a grandmother, after all. "Mark knows what he's doing. There are always two counselors on duty at night, so he's not alone. And the doors are all locked up tight. And, they can call 9-1-1 if anything happens."

"He's supposed to be working in the family firm," Mrs. Russo says as she lifts her eyes to me. "He's had some time to play around like young people like to do, but it's time for him to take his place. His father isn't getting any younger. His father needs him."

The older woman turns back to the police scanner and adjusts some knobs. There is nothing except static, but she keeps turning.

"It's a terrible time for my handyman to be away. I'll have to call the help number myself," she finally says as she looks up at me again. She squares her shoulders. "I'm sorry. I should offer you some tea. It's not often one of Mark's friends comes by."

"Oh, I'm not a friend," I say in a panic. "I work with Mark at the shelter. That's all."

I resist the urge to assure her I don't carry a knife.

"Did he get his books?" Mrs. Russo asks.

"I saw some boxes being unloaded," I say cautiously. I don't like the personal tone the conversation has taken, but there's nothing on my index card to suggest a way to bring it back to what I'm here for so I just keep going. "I know the desk came. And it's a beautiful piece of furniture."

Mrs. Russo nods. "This desk and that one used to be in the family's law offices—Russo and Son." She looks up at me. "Maybe you've heard of it. They specialize in entertainment law. The matching chairs came from the office, too, when they remodeled."

"I didn't know Mark was one of those Russos," I say. Of course, I've heard of the big legal firm on Wilshire Boulevard, west of downtown. They're so large they have their own internship program. Not that I'm looking for an internship, since I'd rather work with the judge, but still it's impressive. I could use some of their castoff furniture, too. I bet their interns don't sit on those plastic office chairs like we do at the judge's.

"He's the son in Russo and Son," Mrs. Russo says almost mournfully. "My husband started the firm and, back then, Mark's dad was the son. After my husband died, my son became the Russo and Mark became the son. Except he doesn't want to have anything to do with the firm."

"Oh, I'm sure he *wants* to," I say. Who wouldn't want a setup in a law firm like that? I figure I'll need to work for ten years after I finish law school to come close to being a partner, and that would be in a little firm, nothing like Russo and Son. "He's just—"

I drift off because I honestly have no idea why Mark is dragging his feet. Maybe he's trying to get better terms. Or a better desk. I don't know. In my opinion, he should be happy with the six-figure salary the firm will no doubt pay him. What am I saying? He'll be an owner in the firm. He can probably decide what to pay himself. I'm sure he's not paid more than thirty thousand to work at the shelter since he gets room and board, too. Refusing to work in the family firm is costing Mark lots of money.

"He needs a girlfriend," Mrs. Russo announces. Her shoulders aren't slumped any longer, and her eyes snap with decision. "There's nothing like a woman to make a man tend to the serious business of life."

I finger the index card in my pocket. Carly and I never even considered that the conversation might go in this direction. "We help dozens of kids every day. I think the shelter *is* serious business."

"Well, of course, you would, dear."

"I know that law is very serious, too." I put on my most studious face. "In fact, I'm going to law school next fall."

Mrs. Russo gives me a suspicious look. "I thought you worked at the shelter."

"I've been volunteering there. It's not my job." I feel a tiny bit disloyal when I say that, but it's the truth.

"I see." Mrs. Russo says as she keeps up the challenging look.

I figure she's trying to mess with my head, so I stare right back at her. I figure this is good training for the courtroom. Or life in general around Los Angeles.

Mrs. Russo looks down first and, when she does, I realize I've probably destroyed any chance that she might give us a donation to fund our prom banquet. I'm surprised when she looks back up.

"You came to ask about something, a party or something."

I nod in relief. This time I pull the index card out of my pocket. I don't care if she thinks I'm odd. I want to at least get my piece said. "It's really more significant than a party. These kids come from all kinds of horrible backgrounds. They feel bad about life and themselves. They need something to help build their self-confidence and give them hope for a better life. That's why we want to give the kids a prom. Well, it'll probably be more like a banquet, because we can't do dates or anything. But—"

"Nobody wants to date anymore," Mrs. Russo interrupts with a little smile.

I'm not sure where she's going with her remark, but I don't want to get sidetracked so I look down at my card. "We're hoping to do something formal. You know the dresses, the shoes, all of it. And an elegant banquet with wonderful food. We want to show these kids that they can have the same kind of high-school experiences that other kids take for granted. We want it to be something the kids in the shelter will remember."

"I'm sure they'll never forget it."

I look up from my cards. I've pretty much run out of points to make. Mrs. Russo doesn't look moved by my speech. I don't know what to do next though, so I just stand here.

"Will Mark be going to this?" Mrs. Russo asks after a moment.

That's the last question I expected, but I nod. "I'm sure he'll be one of the chaperones. He can tell you exactly how any donations were used."

"He looks good in a tuxedo," the woman continues. "It wouldn't be a bad place for him to take a date."

"I suppose he could bring a date if he wanted," I say. In fact, it would probably be a good reality check for all of those impressionable girls. "I'll make sure he knows he can bring someone."

I don't suppose it's my place to tell him that, but I will anyway. I can't quite picture his date, but I'm sure she's a blonde. And pretty. One of those cheerleader types, I think. I force my mind away from Mark and his date. I remind myself that there's still a chance we'll get a donation.

"Oh, he won't ask anyone." Mrs. Russo waves her hand in irritation. "You're going to have to do that for him."

"I beg your pardon?"

Mrs. Russo leans toward me. "It's simple really. I'm prepared to give you a modest donation for your event if, and only if, Mark attends with a date. I haven't been able to get him to go out to any of the events I've chosen for him."

"I can't really speak for Mark." I'm thinking it's time to leave now.

Mrs. Russo waves away my hesitation. "Oh, he'll do it. He'll do anything for those kids. All you have to do is find a sweet girl for him to take. Surely, you have a friend who would enjoy going to this thing with Mark. Preferably someone who isn't already connected to the shelter. He needs to meet more people. Maybe someone in the arts. Men always seem to like the fluffy women."

Barbie-doll women, I think, but I don't say anything. I mentally go through the list of people I know. I don't know any artists.

"I do have a friend who is studying ballet," I say before I can develop a conscience about this. It's not like I'm selling anyone into slavery or anything, I tell myself. I wouldn't call Lizabett fluffy—and she's no Barbie-doll—but she'd probably be excited to go to the prom banquet with Mark. It's not even an intimate date. There's going to be dozens of kids along. Lizabett and Mark probably wouldn't even need to talk to each other if they don't want.

Mrs. Russo nods. "I'll write a check."

"But I have to ask the two people first." I'm getting a little panicked. I wish I had some quick answers on my index card.

Mrs. Russo opens a desk drawer. "You'll make it work."

The deal is made.

I leave Mrs. Russo's house as soon as I can, leaving nothing behind but the business card she has requested. I write my cell-phone number on the card and tell her I won't cash the check until I know our plan has everyone's approval. I tell her I need a go-ahead from Mark and one from my friend, too. Even with the money, I need to play fair.

Mrs. Russo just smiles and folds the check in half before giving it to me.

I don't give in to the temptation to see how much of a

donation she has made. I slip the check into my pocket like I'm not concerned about it at all. I do give a good look around the yard before I step out of the door just in case there is a dog roaming around out there. I definitely wouldn't put it past Mrs. Russo to have a pit bull outside her house. She drives a hard bargain.

When I get in my car, I see that it's not even eight o'clock yet. I feel like I've been up all day and I suspect most people are just opening their eyes. I need to drive back to Carly's so I can pick up my overnight bag and give her the details of my meeting before she heads off to church.

Last night, when we were getting ready for bed, Carly invited me to go to church with her, and I said I would think about it. Marilee has also invited me several times. I am usually not in Pasadena on a Sunday morning, so today just might be the day to make a token visit to the church they both attend. Especially because Lizabett already told them she'd go with them today.

How can I refuse to go when even Lizabett, who is a little shy, is willing to go?

I have learned a lot about what it means to be a friend from the others in the Sisterhood, and I know it is important to understand the various pieces of a friend's life. Like, with Lizabett, I've attended the ballet productions she is in. And, when Carly played Mary in the nativity play, I went to see her even though I was a little upset with her at the time.

Church is just one more activity I will share with the others. I will survive. I'm sure I've been to a Christian church before even if I don't remember it. Someone probably took me when I was in one of my foster homes. I still have a fuzzy association of music with church, so I must have been to church, at some point. I tell myself I will likely enjoy the music even though the rest of it will probably bore me completely.

Then I remind myself that boredom is a suitable penance for taking Mrs. Russo's check. Even if I plan to get everyone's okay, it still feels a little questionable to be a paid matchmaker, especially when I don't even want the two people to make a go of it.

I'm relieved when I can turn the corner onto Washington Avenue and enter Carly's driveway.

Chapter Six

"We are all strangers in a strange land, longing for
home, but not quite knowing what or where home is."
                                        —Madeleine L'Engle

*Lizabett brought us this quote when we were talking
about living with our parents. This was after the worst
of our cancer was over and we were starting to look
around us and see how much of life we had missed while
we were sick. One of the things that bothered Lizabett the
most was that she had graduated from high school and
was still living with her widowed mother. More than any
of us, Lizabett wanted to be independent. Even when we
were declared cancer free, though, we couldn't just start
living our lives by picking up where we would have been
if it weren't for our illness. We needed time to adjust.*

*Lizabett is still living with her mom, just like I'm still
living in my princess-papered bedroom at my parents'
house. Neither one of us is exactly happy about it, but it
is what is.*

I'm sitting beside Lizabett in church. I brought the Sisterhood journal with me, and I set it between us. Somehow it makes me feel like I have an anchor in an alien sea to have it beside me. None of the others seem bothered by the strangeness. Marilee and her boyfriend, Quinn (also Lizabett's brother) are sitting on the other side of Lizabett, and Carly is sitting on the other side of me.

When we first sat down, I felt trapped. The songs that everyone sang made me feel a little more relaxed though until they started singing something about temptation. Then I told myself I deserved to be here and uncomfortable at that.

Light filters in through the stained-glass windows and there is solid wood all around. I've gone to quite a few synagogues in my life, and they use a lot of wood, too. Maybe we have more in common than I thought.

I wonder what Lizabett will say when I tell her about the bargain Mark's grandmother is offering up. Hopefully, the feeling of guilt that is rumbling around inside of me is unjustified. I did tell Mrs. Russo that I wouldn't force Mark or my friend to go through with this date thing. I still have plenty of time to return the check even though I did look at the amount before I went back up to Carly's apartment, and it is twenty-five hundred dollars.

It's hard to say no to twenty-five hundred dollars when I'm not even forcing them into a real date anyway. Of course, maybe I'm rationalizing. Al Capone probably started this way, too, telling himself he wasn't such a bad person since he fed stray cats in the morning before murdering people later in the day.

Just in case, I hope Lizbett is paying attention to what the pastor is saying about the need to show mercy and to be kind.

We're about halfway through the sermon, and I'm thinking things are going pretty well when the pastor starts to talk about family. And he doesn't just talk about nice, rosy families, he talks about broken families. He says something about the longing we all have to belong in a family. I keep my eyes straight ahead because I'm afraid the others are going to look at me as the pastor continues. Now he's talking about what happens when our family fails us and we have no one.

I need to remind myself that I am the Tin Man. All of that tin should protect me. I don't understand how the pastor could know my deepest fears, but he's up there talking about them like it's not news to anyone.

I wonder if Marilee told him I was adopted when I was six years old. I'd been in the foster-care system since I was two. During those four years, I was in some kind of limbo. My mother never gave up her rights to me even if she never came to see me. She finally died of a drug overdose when I was five, which made me eligible for adoption. I can't even remember my mother. Sometimes I thought it was the most painful way to be in foster care. Every day I waited for my mother to come visit me, but she never did. Of course, that was a long time ago. I never talk about her now.

I start getting annoyed with Marilee for telling the pastor about my heartache until I realize she didn't know I was coming here this morning. Only Carly knew, and she doesn't know the pastor well enough to convince him to meddle in the life of a visitor. I was with her every minute, and she couldn't have even made a secret cell-phone call to him without my knowledge. It must just be my lucky day. First Mrs. Russo and now God—both taking shots at me.

I move my eyes away from the pastor and look at the banner that is hanging behind him. There's just one simple word on that banner and it is "Joy." If I look at that, I will think of the Joy at the shelter, and I won't have to listen to the pastor. I shouldn't let him get to me like he does, especially because I have a mother now. And a father, too. My adopted parents are good people. They might not be able to give me that baby comfort I missed before I knew them, but they do their best.

My hand moves a little so that I can touch the Sisterhood journal. It makes me feel warm inside to remember that I have the Sisterhood as well as my parents. I am practically overflowing with adopted family. There is no need for me to feel like I am missing something. I don't need to be a child of God.

I don't realize I'm holding my breath a little until the pastor announces that it's time to sing a final song and I feel myself relax. I don't know the words, but I hum along and sing just out of relief that it's over.

I'll never give Carly or Marilee a hard time about going to church again, not even just in my mind. I think it's rather brave of them. Rose is the only one I've ever let talk to me about the way I feel inside. I had no idea church dealt with so many inside issues.

Lizabett doesn't seem any more anxious to hang around after we've been dismissed than I am. I doubt it's for the same reason though since she has more brothers than she knows what to do with. She's certainly not lacking in genuine born-to-it family.

There's a line of people shaking hands with the pastor, but I nudge Lizabett and we slip over to the left and make for the side door.

"How did he know that about me?" Lizabett hisses at me when we've escaped from the church and are walking down the sidewalk to the parking lot.

"Huh?" I turn to look at her. Her arms are swinging while we walk. She's steamed and she's not holding back.

"When he said that about people who don't like to be dependent on others. The pride thing."

"I don't remember that," I say as we reach the parking lot. We may as well wait here for the others to catch up with us. "I thought he was talking about families."

Lizabett starts to pace in front of me. "Well, in general, but he got his points in there about people who are too proud to accept help."

"I guess I didn't hear that. I was more focused on the—" For some reason I need to swallow.

"Oh." Lizabett suddenly stops her fierce walking and looks at me. "I'm sorry. I didn't think. Well, you shouldn't even listen to him on that. I know you never knew your real father and mother, but you don't need them. Anyone who knows you knows that."

I nod. Lizabett is rather illogical and very comforting at the same time.

"Your adopted parents—in their way—they care about you."

I nod. I feel better. And, it's true.

"And the Sisterhood, well, we'd do anything for you."

I stop and look around. Lizabett and I are alone in the parking lot. I see Marilee and Quinn walking toward us, but they won't be here for a minute or so.

"I might actually have something you could do," I say. I'm almost whispering.

Lizabett looks up.

"It's nothing hard really." I try to make my voice sound normal. "I just need someone to go to a party with someone. Sort of like a blind date."

Lizabett gives me a warrior's smile. "I'm not too proud for that. I don't need to get my own date."

Hi, this is Lizabett. I made Becca give me the journal and I'm writing in it while I sit in the backseat of my brother's car. Quinn is talking to Marilee up front so they don't need me for conversation anyway. I just wanted to write down that I am not—I repeat not—going to go out on a date with Becca's boyfriend. I know he doesn't know he's her boyfriend and I'm not sure she knows it, either, but that doesn't make any difference.

This is not a blind date, it's a trap.

I have seen how many misunderstandings can happen when two girls are both dating the same guy. Not that I'd be dating Mark. And not that he'd probably be smitten with me if I did go out with him. I mean, what are the odds?

But—still.

I look out the car window and see Becca getting into Carly's Jeep. Well, it's really Randy's Jeep, but he put Carly on his insurance so she could drive it. She's saving up for a used car, but she won't have enough money to buy one for several months.

I can't imagine Carly asking me to go on a date with *her* boyfriend. And, if she did, it would even be better for me, because I, at least, know Randy. I don't know this Mark guy, except to know that he is drop-dead gorgeous. Five seconds with him and that much is obvious. I'd be nervous going out with him though, and there would be no point to it anyway because he's *Becca's boyfriend*. Doesn't she know you're supposed to keep a boyfriend to yourself and not just give him away to someone else?

Becca waves to me as Carly starts her Jeep and backs out of the parking space next to us. I look up to the front seat in this car and Quinn and Marilee are talking about something.

"They're going to beat us to the restaurant," I say. We are all going to this Thai place on Colorado Boulevard to eat. I told Becca I would have my answer for her at lunch.

If it was anyone but Becca, I wouldn't even still be thinking about it. It's just that Becca never asks anyone for anything. I would give her one of my kidneys if she asked for it. I would go out with any other guy if she asked me to do it. I just don't want her to end up mad at me, and I think that's what will happen if I go out with Mark.

Oh, she'll say it's okay and that she has no attachment to him anyway. And, I'll say it doesn't matter because I had a good time on the date, but there was no chemistry. And neither one of us will believe the other. I really wish she would ask for a kidney instead.

Or, shoes. I have some really cute shoes I'm thinking

her girls will like. I'll give them over gladly. Maybe I should mention that; she needs shoes.

Finally, my older brother, Quinn, decides it is time to start the ignition on his car and actually pull out of the parking lot. He's certainly slow enough about it. I put the journal away then because my handwriting isn't the best when I'm writing in a moving car. I can't decide whether or not to fold back the pages I've just written so I keep thinking about that the whole way to the restaurant.

We have a few minutes to wait to be seated once we're inside the restaurant and I decide to add a few more thoughts to the journal. I already folded back the pages. I don't have tape or a stapler with me, but the Sisterhood will respect my privacy. I'm going to have to say yes to Becca. She needs me. I can't let her down.

The waiter just came and said our table is ready. So, I'm going to give the journal back to Becca.

I'm doomed.

This is Becca. The six of us are sitting around a big table and ordering the lunch special of pad Thai noodles with shrimp and lemongrass soup. Lizabett just whispered to me that she will go on the prom date if I need her to go.

"But why can't you go?" she asks in a low voice. We are sitting next to each other. "You're just as single as I am."

"I work at the shelter, and his grandmother doesn't think I can lure Mark away from his life there."

"I can't lure him anywhere, either," Lizabett protests. "I'm not even sure I'll be able to think of anything to talk to him about."

"That's okay. He likes mysterious women. Just smile here and there and you won't have to talk."

Lizabett is looking at me like I'm nuts.

But, it's okay. I am feeling pretty good. I wasn't sure who would be harder to convince to go on this date, Mark or Lizabett, so getting half of the team to agree gives me hope.

"Just think about chicken cordon bleu," I say. "The twenty-five hundred dollars Mrs. Russo gave us will buy all the food we need for the banquet."

I already did the math for the food. I figure we'll have ninety-five people coming to the dinner. Randy has offered to help cater a complete chicken cordon bleu dinner for twenty-five dollars a person if he can get some of the students from the Culinary Institute to come help him in the kitchen at the Pews. That includes appetizers and fancy desserts and sparkling water.

Randy owns his own sports diner in Hollywood, but he used to work at the Pews and came back last fall to take over for Uncle Lou for a few weeks so the older man felt free to take his first vacation in years. Randy has been catering several elegant events in San Marino that Carly's aunt set up for him, so I know he'll do a great job. He's already talking stuffed mushrooms.

I don't think the others are listening to me and Lizabett, but suddenly I notice Quinn looking at me.

"You got a donation from Mrs. Russo, after all. Congratulations," he says and he's loud enough for everyone to hear.

"You did it?" Marilee turns to look at me. "I've been wanting to ask, but I figured you might need to set up another meeting with her, and I didn't want to push you."

I force myself to smile. "No, there's no need for us to meet again. I might need to call her, but—no, the check for twenty-five hundred is already in my purse."

"Well, she's got to be a pretty nice lady if she gave the shelter that much money," Carly says. "All for a party. I'm having trouble getting people to donate their old dresses. I can't imagine asking someone for that kind of money. You did good."

"Mrs. Russo has ulterior motives," I say. I glance over at Lizabett. She's looking miserable. "Shall I tell them?"

Lizabett nods.

"Mrs. Russo is giving us the money on the condition that I find a date for her grandson for the event."

"Mark?" Carly asks, bewildered. "He doesn't need someone to find him dates. Has she taken a good look at her grandson lately? He's gorgeous. He could be on one of those dating shows on television."

"Becca, you should go with him," Marilee says. "It'd be perfect."

I shake my head. "It can't be someone who works at the shelter. Mrs. Russo asked me to find a friend to do it."

There's a moment of silence.

"Well, Marilee can't go," Quinn finally says. "She's got plans with me that night."

"We don't even know when we're going to have the prom banquet," I say.

"I don't care. Whenever it is, Marilee has plans with me." Quinn has this stubborn look on his face. "She doesn't like gorgeous men anyway."

Marilee puts her hand over Quinn's. "Well, I do like one gorgeous man pretty well."

Quinn smiles over at Marilee and I swear they forget the rest of us are here.

Lizabett rolls her eyes at me. "I had to ride over with them. Before lunch. I'm surprised I can eat."

I wonder if I'll ever be that besotted with someone. I look at Lizabett and she's looking at them, too. We're both a little jealous, I think.

Not that I have time to be mooning over some future love-of-my-life guy who I haven't even met.

I clear my throat so I get everyone's attention. "I don't need Marilee to go," I say to Quinn. "I already made an arrangement with Lizabett."

Now Quinn looks at his sister. A whole new set of emotions come over his face. "You're sure you're up for that?"

Lizabett nods her head. She doesn't look happy, but she's apparently willing to go on the date.

"Randy and I will be there serving food," Carly says and looks up at Quinn. "It's not like she'll be alone."

"She better not be. A guy named Russo is probably a player."

"You've never even met him," Marilee protests. "For all you know, he could be a nice guy."

Quinn grunts. "You're right. I should go down to the shelter and meet him. I'm not going to have Lizabett going out with someone I don't know at all."

"I'm twenty-two," Lizabett protests. "I can take care of myself."

Quinn just grunts again.

The waiter brings our food, and the conversation dies down a bit. I will have to remember that going to church makes me hungry. I look around the table and wonder if it has that effect on all of the others, as well. Then I look around more carefully. The others might be eating like dock workers, but Lizabett is only picking at her food.

"I could find someone else," I lean over and whisper to Lizabett. "Maybe one of Carly's friends."

Lizabett looks up. "But would they understand?"

"I would tell them about the deal with Mrs. Russo."

"It's not that. What if they decide they—you know—*like* Mark?"

"Oh."

Now it's my turn to look down at my plate. Lizabett is right. I have to set Mark up for a date, but I have no desire to set him up in a relationship. He might never ask me out, but I don't want to ensure that he doesn't. Besides, the girls wouldn't be too happy with me if I let someone snap up Mark. And one of Carly's friends would do her best to lure him into a relationship. Not that I could blame her. Any woman who drew breath would do the same. But, if Mark had the wrong girlfriend, he might leave the shelter. The kids there need him.

I wonder if I should just give back the check. That seems extreme though. Where else would we get money for the food? Even if we end up having it at the Pews, we need food.

I lean over and give Lizabett's shoulders a squeeze. "Maybe Mark will be able to talk his grandmother out of the date part of this?"

Lizabett nods. "Maybe."

I suddenly realize that my hardest hurdle is ahead of me. Mrs. Russo might think that Mark would do anything for the shelter, but I'm not so sure. Maybe we'll have bread and water for our banquet instead of chicken cordon bleu with finger bowls. When did this whole thing get so complicated anyway?

Chapter Seven

"High heels were invented by a woman who had
been kissed on the forehead."
          —Christopher Morley, novelist and poet

*Carly is the most fashionable one of the sisters and I
thought she would have been the one to bring us this
quote, but it was Marilee. When her hair fell out from the
chemo, Marilee started wearing those baseball caps that
her father had given her. She became a total tomboy, but
she said later that inside she longed for high heels and
glamour. Having cancer was hard on all of our dreams.
It made us feel like we needed to hide away instead of
being in the middle of things.*

It's Monday morning and I, Becca, am standing on the
steps in front of the doors to the shelter trying to decide
if I've remembered everything I need to say. I wonder if
Mark's grandmother has already talked to him and told
him that I'm supposed to be arranging a date for him. I

feel a little guilty, but I've put on my legal hat and examined this thing backward and forward and, really, if everyone who's involved knows about it then I shouldn't feel guilty about anything. It's called full disclosure.

I can't stand outside here on the steps any longer without attracting attention, so I pull my key out of my pocket to open the door to the shelter since the doors aren't unlocked until after breakfast.

"Hey, lady."

I have the key in the lock when I hear the voice from the sidewalk behind me and turn around.

A tall black kid is walking down the sidewalk toward me. He's wearing a gray knit cap and a neon orange T-shirt that's frayed around the bottom. When he sees my look, he holds up his hands. "Don't get freaked. I just want you to take a note inside to my girl. You know Cand—eece?"

He draws Candice's name out like it's French or something. I see he has a folded piece of paper in one of his hands and he waves it a little.

"Candice is your girl?" I ask with a frown. I don't want to say it, but I thought Candice was interested in one of the guys inside the shelter. Although, this guy with the fake French accent, might appeal to her just as much as Ricky does.

The kid nods. "She'll want the note."

By now he is close enough to me to hand me the note, and I take it even though I don't know why people keep expecting me to be Cupid.

"Tell her it's from Jason," he says as he starts backing away.

"Okay." I put the note in my pocket.

I keep frowning as Jason turns around and walks away. It's not exactly against the rules for Candice to have a friend who isn't part of the shelter program, but no one encourages the kids inside to mix with their old friends. For one thing, those old friends aren't necessarily making any effort to come clean with drugs and violence.

Of course, I don't have any evidence that Jason is into either one, but he didn't look like he was dressed to be going to school or to a job. I decide I'll have to get more information on him from Candice.

I turn back to the door and finish opening it up. I can tell by the noise that breakfast is still going on. I don't smell the bacon, so it must be cold cereal and toast this morning.

I walk across the lounge to get to the back dining room. I notice Mark's desk chair is pushed against the far wall. The chair's finely polished wood looks out of place in the middle of the surrounding shabby furnishings. I almost stop to see if the chair has been scratched, but I don't. Mrs. Russo didn't send me here this morning to check up on the chair; she sent me here to get Mark to that prom banquet with a date.

I walk through an arch and turn a corner before I see the kids all sitting there. They're a jumble of color and motion and I feel satisfaction seeing them all talking and eating. A couple of the girls look up and smile at me. I see Candice, but I don't wave the note at her. She can finish her cereal in peace.

Mark is sitting at the end of the table and he has his back to me. When he sees the girls looking at a spot behind him, he turns around and sees me.

"Ah, Becca," Mark says as he pushes back his chair. "Just the person I've wanted to see. How'd it go with my grandmother? Did you get a donation?"

"I think so."

Mark stands up and walks toward me. "Don't worry if you don't have the check yet. If my grandmother says she'll send the check, she will. She's good for it."

"Oh, I have the check. I'm just not sure we can keep it."

"Why wouldn't we keep it?" Mark is standing right in front of me now and he's smiling like I've done a good thing. I can see why the girls get so confused with Mark. He's looking at me like I'm the most important person in the room. If I didn't know he looks at everyone that way when he talks to them, I could get confused about his feelings.

I take a deep breath. The conversation at the table is still going on behind him, but I'm focused on Mark. "The check comes with a request. Well, more of a demand, I suppose." I swallow and take one last look at his eyes. "Your grandmother is making the donation if I can make you go to the prom banquet with a date."

The sounds of the table conversation fade.

Mark starts to laugh, deep and low. "That's my grandmother for you."

"You don't mind?"

"Of course, I mind." Mark's laugh quiets to a chuckle. He lowers his voice. "She knows that."

I look at the kids sitting at the table behind Mark and they're not even bothering to pretend they aren't trying to listen.

"She also knows I'm not dating anyone at the moment—"

I see two of the girls high-five each other behind Mark's back.

"So there's no way I've asked anyone to this thing," Mark finishes quietly.

I nod and try to keep my voice low so the kids won't hear. "Your grandmother doesn't think you'll ask anyone, either. That's why she asked me to arrange it."

That takes the last trace of laughter out of Mark's eyes. "I see."

I'm almost whispering now. "I'm glad you do because I don't get it. It's not like you're going to marry someone if you go out with them once anyway so I don't see why—"

"My grandmother mentioned me getting *married?*" Mark says, obviously forgetting anything he may have been thinking about keeping things quiet.

"Oh, no," I say as I motion with my head to the kids behind him. "She just wants you to have a girlfriend so you'll—you know—settle down."

This whole thing is crazy. Mrs. Russo should have known I wouldn't have the finesse to be a matchmaker. After all, I stood in front of her and read from my index card. That should have been a clue that I couldn't wheel-and-deal effortlessly. I've never envisioned myself as a trial attorney. I'm more the "find the right defense" kind of a person. I make a terrible Cupid.

I look at Mark. "Maybe we should go to your office so—" I nod my head in the direction of the kids.

"No," Mark says as he ignores my caution about the

listening kids. Now, this is a guy who would make a good trial lawyer. I see the resolve on his face. A jury would melt about now. "If I'm going to do this, I need to do it right."

Mark breathes deeply. "Becca." He looks down at me and I melt. He pauses and then continues, "Will you go to the prom with me?"

Applause erupts behind us.

For a blinding second, I think I've found my prince. Then reality returns.

"But I can't," I blurt it out. "Your grandmother says I won't count because I work here. It has to be someone else."

"Good. We can't let her dictate everything. It's bad for her character," Mark says and then he bends down slightly and gives me a kiss on my forehead. My *forehead!*

I don't think a prince kisses anyone on their forehead. Even Sleeping Beauty got it on the lips.

A chorus of boos come from behind us and Mark turns around to face the kids. "That's an example of how much kissing will be allowed at this prom banquet thing."

There's shocked silence. I don't hear it at first though because I'm so surprised myself. Did I just get kissed to demonstrate some kind of a lesson?

"You're kidding us, right?" one of the guys finally says. "Nobody kisses a girl on her *forehead*—that's like—"

"It's like an expression of affection," Mark says. "Without being a move."

I can see the twinkle in Mark's eye by now, and I

realize he's having a good time teasing the kids. At least, I think he's teasing.

"But I'm going to be wearing high heels," Candice protests. She's sitting at the table with her empty bowl and glass in front of her. "A forehead kiss is more for—like—tennis shoes."

"Tennis shoes?" Lupe, who is sitting next to her, says with a snort. "More like orthopedic shoes if you ask me. You'd have to be dead and in the casket to like a kiss on the forehead."

Mark shrugs his shoulders. "I guess we can talk about the kissing aspects of things later in group meeting."

The kids groan. They get it.

And, just like that, the whole noise level is back to normal. I've seen Mark bring up topics like this before. He has a way of building up interest in what he wants to talk about later so that everyone comes to group meetings and talks. It appears that even the kids know what he's up to. I suspect a discussion on kissing will only be an introduction to things like STDs and unwanted pregnancies.

At least by now I have my pulse back under control. Fortunately, I don't think anyone noticed my breathlessness.

"You didn't get a chance to answer me," Mark says softly. He's still looking at me. "Would you be willing to go to the prom with me?"

I can think of ten reasons right off of the top of my head why I should refuse. But his eyes are rather nice. Okay, so maybe they're mesmerizing. I find my head nodding a yes instead of a no. I do keep enough sanity to add, "If your grandmother will agree."

Mark grins. "It will be my pleasure to inform her that I've already asked a date to the prom."

"But the check," I say. I know the Sisterhood would be shaking their heads over me about now. This is supposed to be a romantic moment. I shouldn't be thinking about the rules Mrs. Russo put on that check. I can't help myself though. I'm a rules kind of person. Especially now that I've got my breathing under control.

"You can call her yourself after I talk to her just to be sure it's okay," Mark says.

I nod. I'll do that.

"It makes sense for me to go with one of the staff from here anyway," Mark continues. "No real date would have the patience to put up with dozens of kids tagging along."

Well, that wiped the rest of the romance away.

"Of course," I say.

"Not that we won't have fun," Mark adds like he's realized what he's just said.

I smile. "I'm looking forward to it."

I tell myself that it's best that it isn't a real date anyway. I don't have time to have a relationship, or I won't have time this fall when I start law school, so it's best not to start something that would only have to end in a few months anyway. Besides, I'll probably wrap up my volunteering here after the prom banquet and that would make it uncomfortable to see Mark. I'll keep telling myself that, but I don't know if I really believe it. The rest of the reasons escape me. Not that I need to worry about it now. Mark has already walked back to the table, and he's now carrying his breakfast dishes into the kitchen.

I don't have a chance to move before Candice and Lupe come up to me.

"You're going to the prom. You're going to the prom," Lupe sings as she does a little dance around me.

"I was already going to the prom," I say with a smile. "Remember, I'm one of the chaperones."

"But now you're *really* going to the prom," Candice says with a huge smile. "You've got a date."

Fortunately by now, almost everyone has left the dining room and is either in the kitchen or back out in the lounge.

"It's not such a big deal," I say.

Candice gives me a knowing look. "Who do you think you're kidding? After missing your own prom because of the cancer thing. This is a very big deal."

Lupe nods. "You can have the red dress if one comes in. Red's your color."

"And shoes! Girl, we've got to get you some killer shoes," Candice adds.

"Maybe there'll be a backless dress. Something sexy," Lupe says with a dreamy look on her face.

"We'll see if Mr. Mark kisses you on the forehead then," Candice says with a scowl.

"There's not going to be any kissing. Mark and I will both be chaperones and besides—I, ah, he's just doing this to be nice."

Candice raises her eyebrow.

"He wouldn't have asked me if his grandmother hadn't made that crazy request with her check."

"Still, it's you he asked," Candice says stubbornly.

I suppose that is true, although there wasn't anyone else in the room at the time who was both female and an adult. Candice and Lupe might not know it, but Mark would never ask one of the residents to be his date. I'm surprised he even asked a volunteer. Maybe he knows I'm leaving soon.

"We need to get working on the dresses," Lupe says. "We'll want to have them altered before the next shipment comes in. We can only do one or two at a time."

"Candice, wait a minute," I say as Lupe walks off to the lounge.

I hold out the note. "Some guy named Jason gave this to me to give to you."

Candice nods in satisfaction as she takes the note.

"I thought you were interested in Ricky," I say. Ricky is one of the shelter guys and he's actually working on his GED and going to his AA meetings. That makes him a much better person for Candice to know, in my opinion. He even owns a T-shirt that doesn't have holes in it.

Candice shrugs. "A girl can never have too many boyfriends."

"She sure can," I say. "Especially when one of them isn't even addressing his problems."

"You worry too much," Candice says as she starts toward the door heading to the lounge. "Let's go work on the dresses."

I make a note to talk to Candice later, but, for the time being, I walk into the lounge with her.

Over a dozen girls are sitting around the lounge and Lupe is holding up two cream-colored dresses.

Carly has managed to find a total of three dresses so far. The one black dress was put aside yesterday for Joy and today the two ivory dresses will be assigned to two of the younger girls. None of the dresses fit, of course, and that's why all of the girls are in the lounge with boxes of safety pins.

It doesn't take me long to realize that the girls are planning to take some short cuts.

"You can't just make the dresses fit with safety pins," I say.

A dozen pairs of eyes look up at me guiltily.

"That's what we always do with our clothes," Lupe finally says.

"But it won't take that much extra work to sew the alterations properly," I say.

There's a moment of silence before I realize that, of course, none of them know how to sew.

"I'll bring in some needles and thread tomorrow," I say. "It's not hard to learn how to make some simple seams."

There's another moment of silence.

"Could we learn buttons, too?" one of the younger girls asks. "I never have any buttons."

"That's why you wear T-shirts," another girl says. "That way you don't have to worry about buttons."

"Yes, we'll do buttons," I say. "You don't always want to be wearing a T-shirt."

All day I think about teaching those girls how to sew seams and buttons. Rose did a similar thing for the Sisterhood when she taught us all how to knit. I had never realized how satisfying it would be to pass along a sewing skill. I wonder if the girls at the shelter will ever sit around and sew like the Sisterhood sits around and knits. If they do, I wonder if they will become friends like we have.

Chapter Eight

"Don't cry because it's over. Smile because it happened."

—Dr. Seuss

That first year we were together, Rose brought several Dr. Seuss books to our meetings and read to us. It was very comforting. I don't remember anyone ever reading to me as a child. By the time I was adopted, I guess I was too old to be tucked into bed with a story. Still, even today, when I want to snuggle down in my bed and sleep like a baby, I remember those evenings when Rose read to us. I can still see her.

I'm going to write in the journal for a little bit before I go to sleep. This is Becca, and I've sprayed my sheets with some of that lavender scent Carly used on the sheets at her place. She says it's supposed to make a person relax. So far it hasn't worked. I laid down twenty minutes ago, and the lavender scent hasn't even slowed down the racing inside my head, so I got up again.

I'm going on a date with Mark. Me, old Tin Man herself. I don't know if the date will turn out good or bad, but I'm going to give it my best. When I left the shelter around noon today, I called the rest of the sisters right away and told them my news. I called Lizabett first, and I thought she'd hyperventilate while telling me how happy she was I was going with Mark. Marilee and Carly were only slightly more subdued.

It felt good to be wrapped in their joy. For once, I didn't need to look for reasons why something wouldn't work or why we needed to go slow. It had even occurred to me that going with Mark to this prom banquet was about as perfect as a date can be in my life. He will be so busy watching out for the kids that he won't even notice if I don't have enough to say.

I know he only asked me to go with him because of his grandmother, so I have no expectations beyond the night. It takes all of the pressure off. But doesn't keep a small part of me from wishing it was more.

I tried explaining the pressure part of this to the Sisterhood, but I don't think they understood. Carly kept saying I shouldn't give up hope. I told her I wasn't giving up the hope, I was giving up the worry, but I don't think she got it.

I've never really admitted to anyone that I'm a little afraid to date. I don't do so well with emotions, and I worry a guy might be disappointed in me as a date.

Of course, today wasn't the time to tell the sisters that. So I moved on. I assured the Sisterhood that I was still planning to have them come to the prom banquet to help out with everything so, hopefully, no one will feel left out. I can tell they are all getting into the spirit of the thing.

Lizabett and Marilee are even bringing their sewing kits over to the shelter tomorrow morning so they can help me teach the girls how to sew a seam. Carly said she would come, but she's going to make some more phone calls in an effort to find more dresses first. She's not finding as many women willing to part with their finery as she had hoped.

"My aunt says she knows some of these women have dresses in their closets they'll never wear again," Carly told me in frustration. "But they still don't want to give them up."

I tell Carly I'll help her do some calling tomorrow, as well.

Even with writing in the journal, I'm not getting sleepy. (Marilee, if you read this, I don't mean to imply that the journal should be boring—it's just that I expected it to be calming. You know, in a good way. And tonight it hasn't done anything for me in a relaxing way.)

Anyway, I decide a cup of cocoa might help me sleep instead, so I'm going to close up the journal for tonight and go to the kitchen.

I like the house when it's dark and shadows fill the corners. I have the light on over the stove and I pull a small saucepan out of the cupboard so I can boil some water. I try to be quiet, but the sound of running water wakes my mother, and before I know it, I see her in the doorway.

"Problems sleeping?" my mother asks as she yawns and pulls her robe more tightly around her.

"I don't mean to keep waking you up," I say as I glance down at the pan of water that is just starting to boil.

"It's okay," my mother says as she walks into the kitchen. "Are you making cocoa?"

I nod.

"Make some for me, too," she says as she sits down at the table. "We don't have enough time to talk anymore."

I wonder if my mother knows I have something I haven't told her. Somehow I just couldn't tell her that I have a date for this prom banquet and that I'm excited about it. I've told myself since I got home tonight that I'm just waiting to get a clear go-ahead from Mrs. Russo before I tell my parents, but I'm not sure that's all there is to it.

"How are things going with your banquet?" my mother asks.

I look at her more closely, just to see if she suspects something, but she looks too sleepy to be subtle. Besides, that's not my mother's style; she'd just ask outright.

"We're having some problems getting dresses for the girls," I say as I reach into the cupboard and get a couple of mugs.

"I thought Carly was going to find the dresses in San Marino."

I set the mugs on the counter and start to pour hot water into them. "It turns out that the women there don't want to give away their party dresses, even if they don't need them. Carly says lots of the women have dresses in the back of their closets that are way too small and they still don't want to give them up."

My mother smiles. "Maybe the dresses have fond memories for them."

"Still, if someone else could use them."

"The way to get them to part with their dresses is to let them get to know the girls who will be wearing them."

I stir the cocoa into the water and carry the cups to the table. "You mean like sponsorship?"

My mother nods and gets a real sweet look on her face.

I set the cocoa on the table and sit down. "That might work."

I guess I still sound hesitant because my mother continues. "You know, like they do with the starving children. You sponsor a child. You don't just give to a country."

I wonder briefly if that's what my mother did when she adopted me. Seeing me as a child instead of a statistic. I turn my thoughts back to the prom banquet though. "Maybe it would work. We could take pictures and have the girls write letters."

"Or," my mother says and then takes a sip of cocoa. "You could just introduce some of the girls to the women with the dresses. That's the best way."

"Some of the girls are a little rough around the edges."

My mother shrugs. "If the women have a heart, they'll see past that."

All I can do is nod and drink some of the cocoa myself. "I'll talk to Carly about it tomorrow."

My mother and I drink our cocoa and then head off to bed. At least worrying about the girls meeting those women from San Marino takes my mind completely off my date with Mark so I go to sleep easily. I don't count sheep, but I do keep seeing a red prom dress swirling around in my dreams. I think Lupe is chasing it.

I drive to the Pews the next morning and open the diner to the smells of breakfast. It smells like coffee and sausage and these special breakfast biscuits that Uncle Lou makes with cheddar cheese and jalapeños.

"Hi," Uncle Lou calls to me as he walks past with a coffeepot. "I'll catch you on the way back if you want something to open your eyes."

"That'd be great. Thanks," I say as I sit down at the counter. I'm not sure if he's talking about his biscuits or his coffee. Those jalapeños are something.

Carly comes out of the kitchen with two orders of pancakes on platters she's carrying.

"I'll be back," Carly says as she walks past me to the table she's serving.

I can't help but notice how happy Carly seems. Not that working as a waitress is her goal in life. But working in the Pews means she can be independent and support herself. Carly likes being able to do that.

I wondered this morning as I drove into Pasadena if I will ever be independent like Carly and Marilee. I know everyone expects me to set up my own apartment the minute I get my scholarship money to start law school, but I'm not so sure anymore. The closer the time comes, the more I drag my feet. I will miss having cocoa with my mother in the middle of the night for no reason except that I can't sleep. I guess I'm just not in as much of a hurry to be independent as the others in the Sisterhood think I am.

Carly comes back to my table with her order pad. "What'll it be?"

"A toasted bagel and coffee."

"Well, that's easy," Carly says as she makes a mark on

her order pad and puts it back in her pocket. "So what's up?"

"My mother thinks we should get sponsors for the girls for the prom banquet. You know, like they do with the starving children in Africa where you give money to a particular child."

Carly nods.

"My mother thinks the women would give away their dresses if they knew the girls who were going to be wearing them."

Carly nods again. "That's not a bad idea."

"Except that the girls, well—can you see them sitting down to tea with your aunt's friends?"

"Well, we want the girls to have new experiences," Carly says with a shrug. "And it would do my aunt's friends a world of good to see that everyone doesn't live the kind of life they do."

"I wouldn't want—" I swallow. "It's just that I don't want the girls to feel awkward, like they're on some kind of a display."

"No one will look down their noses at your girls," Carly says. "I'll make sure my aunt understands not to invite that kind of woman."

"Good." I don't want any of the girls to be ashamed of who they are. Pride is all some of them have. "And all the girls should have a sponsor. We'll have to set it up that way."

Carly leaves to do her waitress thing and I sit there for a minute before pulling out the journal.

This is Becca and I want to write a few words about independence. I'm still thinking about Mark's grandmother. I never realized that most people my age are caught in webs of worry. Mark has his grandmother and his father to worry about him. Carly has her parents and sometimes her aunt and uncle. Marilee has her mom and Lizabett has all her brothers.

I don't think any of them appreciate the worry they get since they've had it all of their lives. If they were late getting home from school, someone would worry. If they couldn't sleep, someone worried. No matter what turn they took in their lives, someone would care.

The girls from the shelter could tell them what a rare, precious thing that web of worry is.

I don't have any real memories of my life before I was three and went to my first foster home, but I have a feeling deep in my bones that no one cared about me. Maybe the reason I am so much like the Tin Man is because I had no one to love me in those early years. I've always assumed I was living with my mother until I went to the foster homes, but I don't know for sure. If I was, she must have been hooked on drugs most of that time. She might have gone into treatment for a time though, I tell myself. Maybe that's why she couldn't come and visit me.

I know this all seems like weighty words to put down in the journal when I haven't even had my breakfast. I'm sure Lizabett would say I just had low blood sugar. But I want to write it down before my courage escapes me. There's something so naked about admitting that I know I wasn't loved as a young child. I've always just told myself that I didn't know if I had anyone to hug me back then because I don't get any mental pictures when I try to remember those days. I wouldn't recognize a picture of me or the house I lived in back then. There were certainly no images of my mother.

I feel a big huge hole where that memory should be.

Sometimes, I think I'm not a Tin Man at all. Maybe I am a black pit instead. When I first came to live with my adopted parents, I had to adjust to more than the princess wallpaper. I didn't know what to do when my mother hugged me, either. I just held myself rigid and didn't breathe. I was so afraid of doing the wrong thing. It took me a few times to learn to hug her back and, even then, I gave tentative hugs.

The one vague wisp of a memory I do have of my early days is of me lying with my face to the wall and crying silently in the night. Whoever was there with me in the darkness got angry with me if I cried. I knew that so I clenched my jaw together so that no sobs escaped. I always told myself that maybe that person in the dark was not my real mother. Maybe my mother left me with a babysitter some nights.

I still sleep facing the wall of my bedroom. And, sometimes when I wake up, my jaw is clenched.

Oh, I see Marilee coming in the door to the Pews. I'm going to put the journal aside now. I think I'll fold these pages back for a little bit, just until the rawness in the back of my throat goes away. I wouldn't want Marilee to read them quite yet and I know she'll want to add something to this journal.

I might tell her that I've given up on writing down rules though. I never realized how seductive it is to write in the journal. It's like crying without making any sound. I can write down things in the journal that I could never tell someone face-to-face.

I wonder if Marilee and Carly felt that same way when they had the journal.

Chapter Nine

"I was like a hit album waiting to be released. I knew my day would come."

—Oprah Winfrey

In the early days of the Sisterhood, we used to love stories of people who had overcome great things. We loved to watch Oprah on television because she often had these people on her show. Rose brought us this quote one evening and told us that we each had great things to look forward to in our lives.

I'm not sure if we all believed Rose. I know I didn't. By then, though, I had learned to keep some of my pessimism to myself. I told myself that maybe things would turn out okay for the rest of the Sisterhood. I believed that the one of us with the most dropped stitches was me. I was the one who didn't deserve to make it, not even when I was trying my best.

Carly's aunt already had plans to host a meeting of the San Marino House and Garden Club when Carly mentioned our idea to her of a one-on-one sponsorship of the girls to get them ready to attend our prom banquet.

"My aunt said the women will love it," Carly says. She's standing in the kitchen at the Pews with a metal spoon in her hand. She's making a batch of chocolate bread pudding. I (Becca) am filling salt shakers and Lizabett and Marilee are cutting up tomatoes and pickle spears for the hamburgers. We all have, on occasion, waited tables at the Pews so we know our way around the place.

"You're sure none of the women will make the girls feel bad about themselves?" I ask for the tenth time. Carly has assured me that her aunt has changed dramatically, but I still remember the way she used to treat Carly. I don't want anyone to be rude to any of the girls. Candice has her pride. And I wonder what the women will make of Lupe's missing tooth. Will they see past her imperfections to her warm heart?

"My aunt was clear with everyone that the girls were to be treated like family," Carly says.

Lizabett winces. "Maybe if she just emphasizes respect that would be better. The girls don't want to be bossed around."

"Nobody does," Marilee adds.

Carly nods. She looks confident. "My aunt understands and she can be firm with the others."

No one questions that Carly's aunt can be firm. We've seen her in action.

"Well, then." I take a deep breath and screw the lid on my last salt shaker. "I guess it's a go."

"The club meeting is on Thursday, so we'll have to tell Rose we're not having our meeting at the Pews," Carly adds as she reaches up to pull a glass pan off the shelf. "We won't get any knitting time in, but we can meet for a little after the girls are gone."

"Won't we need to drive the girls back to the shelter?" Marilee asks.

"Oh, I didn't think of that." Carly pours the bread pudding mixture into the pan. "How many trips will we have to make? I can only get three others in Randy's Jeep."

"I can take four," Marilee says.

Lizabett's car is in the shop so I know she's not available.

"I can take three," I say. "So I think we'd need to make several trips each."

"We can skip a Sisterhood meeting since it's for the girls," Lizabett says. "It's not like we always need to meet every week."

Lizabett, Carly and Marilee all look at me.

I know they're expecting me to protest. I am the one who enforces rules like this. But not this time.

"Thanks," I say instead of what they're expecting. "I appreciate your help with the girls."

Marilee smiles. "Well, we have a heart, too."

Lizabett and Carly beam at me. Full wattage smiles light up the kitchen. They are, of course, marking this day and it all has to do with why they think I am doing what I'm doing for the girls.

"I'm responsible for them," I say. "That's all."

I see the smiles slowly fade.

"But you like them, right?" Lizabett asks anxiously. She's stopped smiling completely. "You care about them."

"Of course she does," Marilee answers on my behalf.

I nod to make Lizabett feel better.

There's an awkward silence and then Carly speaks, "We'll want to be sure to record this event in the journal. I think other groups might learn something from this."

Marilee nods. "That's true. There are a lot of non-profit groups for cancer patients. Maybe someone else could use our approach to get their own donations if we leave a detailed report."

"I can do that," I say. I have the journal in my bedroom anyway.

No one says anything else to me about having a heart, but no one moves away from the counter in the kitchen, either.

"I'll pray about everything," Marilee finally says.

"Me, too," Carly adds.

Lizabett and I look at each other. We've already been through a few awkward moments today.

"Well, I better go," Lizabett says.

"Oh, I didn't mean I was going to pray *now*," Marilee says, sounding horrified. "I mean later, before I go to bed. You don't have to leave."

Lizabett stops in the middle of untying her apron. She looks too stricken to say anything.

"We're not opposed to your praying, Marilee," I say softly. "We're glad you pray."

Lizabett nods. "I just need to get home. That's all. I'm going to give my mom a perm. Her hair's a mess."

Marilee nods, but she doesn't look reassured. Maybe

none of us are as carefree as we try to be. I can't stand to see Marilee look vulnerable so I put my hand on her arm. Before I know it, we're all wrapped up in a four-way hug. It feels good and I wonder afterward if I was really the one who made the first move. It seemed like I was, but it couldn't have been. I seldom offer to hug anyone. I must have just thought I was reaching for Marilee when she was reaching for me.

I'm still thinking about that hug when I lie on my bed, facing the wall, and wondering what it feels like to be Marilee and be able to talk to God when you're alone in the dark. I don't like the dark so much. I feel that vague memory come back of someone being mad at me if I lie in my bed and cry in the night.

Thinking about those long ago days makes me uneasy, so instead I try to picture the girls in the dresses we hope they'll have. I know Lupe wants a red dress. I think Candice wants something metallic that shines with sequins. I go to sleep thinking of colored satin and gold sequins.

Thursday evening came faster than I thought it would and I, Becca, am charged with writing all about the sponsorship meeting in the Sisterhood journal. I came to Carly's aunt's place early so that I could help set things up—the chairs, the food and the background music. Of course, when I got there, the maid had everything set up. I don't know of anyone except Carly's aunt who has a maid. Well, unless you count Mrs. Russo, Mark's grandmother. Not that I know her exactly, but I did call her to make sure I would qualify as a date for Mark for the prom banquet. She told me I would do fine. I couldn't tell if she was happy about it, but I was glad she was going to honor her check.

She asked how everything was going and I told her about the sponsorship idea. Before I knew it, I had invited her to come and sponsor a girl, too. I thought she'd be too busy listening to her police scanner to come, but she said she'd like to be there. So now I have to keep an eye out for her tonight, as well.

I am taking a minute to write in the journal before the girls get here. I told Mark about our plan to make several round-trips in our vehicles to get the girls and then take them back. Fortunately, he told me he had taxi vouchers to send the girls back and forth to Carly's aunt's house. The more I see of what Mark has to do to keep the shelter running smoothly, the more impressed I am with him.

I think I hear a taxi driving up now so I'll stop the journal for a minute while I go greet the girls. I hope they're not nervous about meeting the San Marino women. I think about it a second. Of course they're nervous. I can hardly stand the tension myself. Maybe I should hand the journal off to Marilee for a bit. She might put down a prayer if she has to write something. I think we could use it.

I don't get the journal to Marilee before the first group of girls is knocking at the door. The maid is, of course, walking toward the door to open it, and I want to be there. I should have warned the girls about the maid. It's not every day any of us see a maid dressed in a black uniform with one of those white aprons.

Lupe is the first one to enter the door when the maid

opens it. I don't think she even notices that the woman standing there is a maid. Lupe's eyes go right to the ceiling. "Wow! It's like a basketball court in here. How high up does that go?"

"Forget about the basketball court," Candice says as she comes into the house. "Feel this carpet."

"Rugs," the maid says with a smile. "You're standing on handwoven imported Persian carpets."

We're all standing in an entry that is worthy of a king.

"You mean people weave all those little threads together?" Candice says as she looks down at her feet. "I thought they had machines for those kinds of things."

The maid shrugs. "It's a craft. Some people still practice it."

By then the rest of the girls are coming in the door, and the crowd moves Candice and Lupe farther into the house. I see that all of the girls have their hair combed and are wearing jeans or cotton skirts. We had asked them not to wear shorts, and they have honored that. I tell myself that maybe there is hope for the evening yet.

Mark is the last one to come in the door. I hadn't been expecting him, but I'm glad he's here.

"Thanks for coming," I say.

"I thought after you invited my grandmother, I better come and referee."

"I was surprised she wanted to sponsor a girl. I mean, she's already paying for the food."

Mark nodded. "That's my grandmother. She throws herself into projects and there's no stopping her."

I hear the girls behind me and can tell they are all in the main living room by now. Carly's aunt has a Picasso on the left wall, but no one is squealing about that yet. Then I realize they probably wouldn't even recognize the painter's name.

"I hope the girls do okay," I say. I should have given them a quick art-appreciation lesson just in case someone else mentions the painting.

"They will," Mark says as he looks around. Carly's aunt has decorated with shades of gray and a dark teal. "From what I heard, you told them everything they need to know for tonight."

"We did some role playing," I admit. "Lizabett did most of it."

I never knew Lizabett could act so haughty; she played a Lady-of-the-manor for the girls while the rest of us in the Sisterhood taught them to hem a dress. "I think they're ready to meet the Queen if necessary."

Mark smiled. "Even I'm not ready for that and I've had my grandmother to train me."

For the first time, it occurs to me that Mark never talks about his dad when it comes to things like this. It's always his grandmother. I'm going to ask him about that sometime. Not now, of course. Candice is still talking about all the poor people who have to make these carpets and speculating that they must have been slaves. I have a feeling Mark and I are needed in the main living room.

Candice is kneeling down and running her hands over a large rug with deep teal and charcoal tones. "Imagine doing this by hand. Each thread just so. No one would do that by choice. I know how hard sewing is."

"What are you saying? You can't sew," another girl, Marsha, says.

"Can, too. I'm learning." Candice stands up. "You're just jealous because Jason likes me."

Mark steps between the two girls. "You're both learning. And I know you'll do a fine job on any dress you might receive. And you both have better things to think about than boys."

"Ain't nothing better than our guys," Marsha says.

Candice grunts and then looks at Mark.

"You can worry about your guys later," Mark says firmly. "After you get yourselves figured out."

"Besides, you've already got Ricky," Marsha mutters to Candice. "Nobody needs two guys."

There was enough noise with the chatter of the other girls that I don't think Carly's aunt or her maid noticed anything, especially because they have gone off to the kitchen.

I ask all the girls to be seated. "We've got some rules for tonight. Rule number one is no fighting."

I wait for everyone to find a chair and nod at me. I notice that Mark guides Marsha and Candice to different areas of the living room.

"Rule number two is that no one tries to take someone else's dress. The ladies will give the most appropriate dress they can to the girl whose name they draw out of the bowl there."

Everyone looks over to the big crystal bowl with all of the thin strips of paper that is setting on top of the grand piano. We had thought of letting the girls and the women get to know each other and pick each other, but we feared that would be even more awkward for the girls than it already is.

"Rule number three is that no one has seconds on refreshments until everyone is served."

I saved the refreshment rule for last because I know it will arouse the most interest. Until now, the girls didn't know there would be food and all of the kids at the shelter are serious about eating. I never hear anyone joking about what's for dinner.

Just then, the maid rolls in a cart that is loaded with various kinds of cheesecakes.

I think it's the cheesecakes that give the girls courage to interact with the women when they arrive.

"Raspberry white chocolate," I hear Marsha mention to the San Marino woman sitting next to her. Marsha speaks with a natural authority on the subject. "Those two flavors blend perfectly."

"I like it plain," the woman says. "But with a topping of fresh raspberries."

They both have intent looks on their faces.

"Oh, that sounds good, too." Marsha sounds like she's forgotten about Jason. "Any kind of berries are good with cheesecake."

I make the rounds and listen to other conversations. Some of the women are telling stories of their own proms, and the girls are listening closely.

"But what kind of shoes did you wear?" Candice asks the woman who drew her name.

"Strapless heels," the woman says. "Dyed in a copper tone to match my dress. They had a brass buckle on them with little ridges. The ridges were the color of steel rivets. I've still got them."

Candice sighs with a look of pure satisfaction on her

face. "That would make any guy stop and pay attention. Guys love metal."

I look over and see that Marilee has found some time to start writing in the journal. I'd managed to slip the notebook to her when the drawing was taking place. By now, all of the girls have a sponsor.

Hi, this is Marilee. I feel like I'm at a garden party. Carly's aunt has filled her living room with huge bouquets of long-stemmed roses of many colors. They must be from the flower garden she keeps out behind her house. I've never seen such bright yellows and deep dark reds in bouquets together. The flowers are very striking. Maybe it's because the cream and pastel pink roses fill out the range of colors so they are some vivid roses and some pale ones all together.

I'm taking a couple of minutes to write in the journal so that we have a record of this evening. First, I'm going to describe how the room looks. I think this might be useful for anyone who might try to duplicate our program. Atmosphere is important. There are crystal chandeliers overhead that would do justice to a hotel lobby. Everything gleams—the crystals, the glass cups sitting there ready for punch, the polished surface of the piano.

I don't get the full sweep of the room completed before I see Lupe. She's standing beside a bouquet and, at first, I think she's taking deep breaths of the rose-scented air. Then I wonder if she's trying not to hyperventilate. She looks pale. All of the other girls are talking to their San Marino ladies and I notice that Mrs. Russo, the woman who picked Lupe's name, is over by the grand piano talking to Carly's aunt.

I was afraid something like this might happen.

In all of the role-playing, Becca never covered the possibility that one of the women would completely reject the girl whose name she had drawn.

I need to talk to Becca. She knows how difficult Mrs. Russo can be. I'm glad Mark is here. Maybe he can talk to his grandmother.

I, Becca, am sitting in an upright chair and trying not to interfere, even though I think Marsha should find something else to talk about besides cheesecake, and I wish Candice would stop slipping her feet out of her shoes and rubbing them against those Persian rugs. She's looking at the rugs so closely, I wonder if she's checking the fibers for the blood of slave fingers.

I wish I could forget about the girls for a minute and think of something to say to Mark who is sitting beside me. I guess the girls aren't the only ones who have found their grab bag of conversational tidbits to be a little emptier than they had hoped.

"Becca," Marilee comes up beside me and whispers.

I look up at her, happy to see her because she might have some thoughts I could use to carry on an intelligent conversation.

"What's up?" I say, hoping she'll mention a current event that still has some mileage on it.

"I think Lupe has been abandoned," Marilee whispers to me.

Of course, Mark is sitting right here so he hears it, as well. He looks over at Lupe. "Did she tell you that?"

"She didn't need to," Marilee says as she jabs her

finger to her left. "See her over there all alone, looking scared and nervous."

Mark and I are both looking at where Marilee is pointing. I have to agree Lupe doesn't look happy. Usually, she's all grins and giggles.

"Maybe she doesn't like cheesecake," Mark says.

"She already ate her cheesecake," Marilee says. "Not a crumb left."

"I'll go see what's wrong," I say as I start walking across the room. Mark and Marilee trail along behind me.

"Isn't my grandmother her sponsor?" Mark asks as we walk.

"I think so," Marilee says.

"How's it going?" I ask Lupe when I get to the corner where she's standing. I notice Mrs. Russo is still talking to Carly's aunt. I should have thought of this. Carly's aunt prepped all of the women from her garden club. She didn't have a chance to give any instructions to Mark's grandmother though, so the older woman doesn't know she's supposed to be nice.

Lupe shrugs. "Okay, I guess."

"If you want a new sponsor, just let me know," I say even though we already have more girls than we have San Marino ladies. Some of the women are sponsoring two girls. I don't turn around to see what Marilee and Mark think of my rash offer.

"Could I?" Lupe asks as she looks at me with hope on her face. "That woman wants to take me to a dentist."

"Oh." I don't know what to say now.

"My grandmother's going to get you a new tooth?" Mark asks.

Lupe nods. "That's what she said."

"Wow," Mark says. "That'll be great."

"But I hate going to the dentist. You have to wait there all alone and all they have are sports magazines to read and—"

"I'll go with you," I say.

"Really?"

I nod. I'm not sure how I'll manage dental appointments once I am back in my internship, but I'll find a way. I may not always express my emotions, but I do know how to stand by somebody in a doctor's appointment. "Just let me know the time as far in advance as you can."

"She said she wants me to have the tooth before this prom thing," Lupe says. "That's why she's talking to Carly's aunt. They need to think of a dentist who will do an implant."

"I might know one," Marilee says. "We have a dentist who comes into the Pews regularly. He might work you in."

Marilee walks over to the piano to talk with Carly's aunt and Mrs. Russo.

"All I wanted was a red dress for the prom," Lupe says after a minute. "I can get by without a tooth."

I don't tell Lupe, but she can use a tooth a lot more than she can use a red dress. I've been worried about Lupe's missing tooth. I know it will reduce her chances for jobs when she starts looking for one. It isn't fair, but people are often judged by their looks and teeth are so obvious

"Be sure and tell Mrs. Russo thank you for thinking of a dentist," I say. "She's offering more than we even asked."

Lupe nods. "I know. She said she'd get me the red dress if I went along with getting the tooth. I guess she's all right."

Mark and I stand with Lupe for a few more minutes and then we see that his grandmother is coming back so we walk over to an alcove that is filled with potted plants.

"Don't worry," Mark says to me as he motions to one of the straight back chairs lined up next to the wall in front of us. "My grandmother will have Lupe eating out of her hand."

"You're fortunate to have a grandmother like her." I sit down. It's quieter in the alcove and, as long as we're sitting along the wall, the plants hide the rest of the room from our view.

Mark slides his chair close to mine and sits, as well. "My grandmother likes to get her own way, but she has a good heart."

I smile. I'm glad Mark is fond of his grandmother, but I'm even more excited that he pulled his chair close to mine. The chairs were two feet apart. Now, they're more like six inches. Yikes, this is close.

"You've got a good heart, too," Mark says as he then turns his chair a little so he can look at me while he talks. "You did great with Lupe."

"Oh, well, it's nothing. I'm just—" I can't help but notice that our knees are bumping a little.

Mark's eyes are warm. "I know you don't think so, but no one does the things you have been doing unless they care about others."

"I—ah—I wanted that reference," I remind him. "For law school."

I'm getting a little flustered, but I don't want to misrepresent myself.

"You had a reference just by showing up and talking to the girls. This whole prom thing—that's way beyond what you had to do for a reference."

"Well, it hasn't worked out yet."

Mark laughs. He's still looking at me like I'm someone special. "It'll work out. And the girls are very thankful. They might not be saying anything to you, but I hear them at the dinner table. It's 'Becca this' and 'Becca that'. I hope they've told you how grateful they are."

I shake my head. "But that's okay. Sometimes it's hard to say thank you to people."

"I know. I've had to work through that with my own family. They gave me so much and I didn't feel I deserved any of it."

"You're breaking your grandmother's heart by not joining the family firm."

"I want to build something of my own."

I nod. I really wish I had time to think of some safe topics to bring up. Since I don't, I have to go with the truth. "It seems like my parents give me everything, too. I mean since I am adopted. I'm not entitled to any of it. So I just felt guilty when they kept giving me things and more things."

I'm surprised that it's actually a relief to tell someone.

"You know how it all feels then," Mark says.

I nod, and we sit there for a minute in silence. I can't believe Mark and I have something so deep in common.

"I still need to give my parents a proper thank you." I finally say as I hear the rustle of the leaves behind me.

"Becca? You back here?" I hear Candice saying. "You've got to see these shoes."

I turn my head.

"Oh," Candice says as she stands there with some high heels in her hand and a look of horror on her face. "I'm sorry."

"That's okay," I say. "Those are great shoes."

"I didn't mean to interrupt anything. It's just my sponsor had the shoes in her car and she went to get them for me. And I couldn't wait—I'm sorry."

Candice looks deflated.

"Don't worry about it. We were just taking a break," Mark says as he stands. "I suppose we should go back though."

"Yeah," I agree as I stand up, as well. I walk over to Candice. "Let me see those shoes close-up. They're awesome."

"Aren't they?" Candice says, regaining her enthusiasm.

I think of that conversation with Mark when I get home that night. I still haven't told my mother that I'm going to the formal banquet with a date. Or that I'll be all dressed up in something elegant. I decide I'll tell her tonight, but she doesn't come down to the kitchen even though I make myself a cup of cocoa and take longer than usual to drink it.

If I wasn't hoping my mother would show up, I would have pulled out the journal and finished writing about the evening. But the journal is on my bed beside my purse and I am settled into my chair and I have my cup of cocoa in front of me.

In the swirl of gratitude thinking, I promise myself that someday I will thank my parents for adopting me. I have never said it in actual words. I must have thanked them a thousand times for other things, but not for the big one.

Fortunately, the girls did better than that tonight. I think Mark maybe said something to them earlier, because I heard them all thanking their sponsor for helping them get ready for the prom banquet. Candice gave her sponsor a particularly heartfelt thank you, and I noticed she was carrying a bag with those high heels in it. I wondered if her sponsor had promised her a dress to match.

I drink the last of my cocoa and turn the light off in the kitchen before I walk down the hall to my bedroom.

I wonder if I should mentally thank that person in my long-ago past who got angry when I cried. Even with all of the anger, someone must have fed me in those years. And I did have a bed to sleep in. And a wall to face toward. I never remember being homeless. That person had to have been my birth mother. Maybe, if I could feel thankful to her, even for a minute or two, I could move past the lump in my throat and say thank you to my adoptive parents. Maybe my birth mother did the best that she could if she was fighting drugs. Maybe she always meant to visit me.

Chapter Ten

"The bitterest tears shed over graves are for words
left unsaid and deeds left undone."
                                    —Harriet Beecher Stowe

*Rose brought this quote to the Sisterhood, and I always
thought she brought it for me. Of all of the sisters, I was
the one who had the most reason to say something to
someone. My new parents had given me everything, and
I stood before them mute when I should have been saying
thank you every day of my life. Rose knew this.*

*When I said something to the others in the Sisterhood
meeting, Lizabett patted my knee and told me that she
knew how I felt. She called it being over-gifted and said
she sometimes felt that way around her older brother,
Quinn. When someone gives you so much, she said, it's
easy to turn resentful even if you want to be grateful.*

*That wasn't exactly how I felt. I didn't know how to
tell the others how unworthy I felt to receive all the generosity my new parents had given me, so I kept silent. I*

never really believed my parents would have intended all of those good things for me if they knew who I was inside. I kept waiting for them to realize I wasn't the child they thought I was. It was more than the pink princess thing, but that's where it started. I felt like an imposter. My birth mother knew me better than my new adopted parents. My birth mother knew I couldn't obey all of the rules. I was messy and stupid. I didn't deserve a visit or a pink princess on my wall; I would only fail the princess like I failed everyone else.

I sat up in bed the next morning and remembered that quote from Rose. My old feelings of inadequacy surrounded me, but I fought back. It means a lot to me that Mark said he thinks I have heart. I might not be the child my adoptive parents deserve, but I don't intend to wait until I face death again to say a proper thank you to them. That conversation with Mark has been spinning around in my head. I don't think I'd ever told anyone about my reluctance to say thank you to my parents and had the other person really get it. Mark understood even better than the Sisterhood what I meant.

It was odd since Mark was a rich kid and I was born with nothing. I would have thought we would be in opposite corners, but he said we were the same inside. It didn't matter how much we had, he said, it was the magnitude of the gift received that made it awkward. He had been given everything just like I had been, and he had a hard time saying he was grateful. Like me, the whole thing made him nervous.

He and I had talked a little while the girls went to their

taxis. Mark told me he had wanted to earn his position in life and not just have it all handed to him on a silver platter. No one could control a silver platter, he said. I knew what he meant. If I earned something, I felt the universe owed it to me in a way that it didn't owe me if it was served up without any effort. If I earned it, that meant I could keep it.

I don't know why it seems so important for me to say the big thank you to my parents all of a sudden. Up until now, I've managed to skate past it pretty well with words that sound almost the same. It hasn't really been an issue in my life for a long time.

I'm blowing my hair dry when it hits me that the reason being thankful is on my mind is because of Marilee's prayers. She's always bowing her head before she eats to say thank you to God. And, when something good happens, she thanks God right then and there. She's always thanking Him for something.

It was a bit unnerving until I got used to Marilee doing the thanking thing. I still think it's courageous of her. When she says thank you like that to God, she focuses His attention on her. I keep wondering what would happen if He never intended to do her any favors. What if the crumbs just fell from His napkin when He stood up from the table and she's standing below Him thinking His crumbs were intentional gifts to her?

Maybe if she says something about the crumbs, He will take them away.

That's part of my problem.

What if I start thanking my parents for adopting me and I find out that they didn't really intend to do it? Like, maybe, they were looking for another child and I came to them through some kind of bureaucratic mix-up and they were too kind to return me? What if they regret they got me instead of some princess girl?

That's the problem with saying thank you. It puts a lot of focus on the whole situation and I might find out things I don't want to know.

In the past, when I've been up against a challenge like this, I get it over with as fast as possible. That way I don't have to fret about it. As I stand in front of the mirror and comb my hair, I tell myself that's what I'm going to do with this thank you business.

I decide to wear a white blouse and black slacks today. It's what I wear when I go in to work at my internship with the judge and I want to look official when I say my piece. I am up a half hour early, and I should have time to make my parents breakfast before they come down the stairs.

I smell coffee when I open my bedroom door. I walk down the hall to the kitchen and see my mother standing at the counter in her bathrobe. Her dark hair is tousled, and she's not wearing any makeup. She yawns.

"I thought I'd make breakfast for you and Dad this morning," I say. I do that frequently enough that it's not cause for great comment. They both like my French toast.

"That'd be nice," my mother says as she opens an overhead door, "but your father had to go to work early today. The regional sales manager is coming to the office."

My father is the assistant manager at an appliance store in Glendale. Refrigerators, stoves, that kind of thing.

I decide I'm not going to say my thank you twice, so

I'll wait until my parents are both together. I do have something else to talk about so I go with Plan B.

My mother brings a cup down from the overhead shelf.

"That's okay," I say. "That gives me some time to tell you about the prom banquet."

My mother starts to pour coffee into the cup. "Was last night a success then?"

I nod. "All of the girls have sponsors and we should have the dresses this weekend. Saturday night is the sewing party to do the hems and any alterations that we need. No men are allowed since the girls don't want the guys to see their dresses until the big night."

My mother turns to me with a quick smile. "Good for them."

Then she turns back, takes her cup of coffee and walks over to the table. I follow her.

"After you left yesterday, I wished I had told you to save a girl for me," my mother says as she sits down and then takes a sip of coffee. "I'd love to dress a girl for the event."

"You can dress me," I say as casually as I can manage while sitting down at the table, too. "I even sort of have a date."

My mother sets her cup down and lights up.

"It's more of a business date than anything," I say so she doesn't get too excited.

"Is he wearing a tuxedo?"

"I think so."

"Then we're going all out." My mother reaches behind her to the corner of the cupboard and takes hold of a pencil and a small tablet.

"We don't need to do that."

"Oh, yes, we do. We're going shopping tomorrow morning for a dress. We're not going to waste a guy in a tuxedo."

I haven't seen my mother so excited for a long time so I just grin. She opens the tablet and entitles a page "Stores."

If shopping will do that for my mother, then shopping it is. I have enough in my savings to cover a dress. We spend some time talking about what stores we have to visit. It's too bad my mother couldn't have been a general; she would have done a good job. Fortunately, she seems to take my word when I tell her the date part isn't any big deal. She's just happy to have someone in formal dress escorting me to the event.

Both of my parents have actually been pretty good about me and dating. They don't rush me at all. They say I should look around and be very picky. That's just one more thing that's kind of nice about them and something I should thank them for. I know it will make my prom banquet date more relaxed.

After I finish talking to my mother, I go back to my bedroom and take the Sisterhood journal out of the big purse I have. I don't bother writing any introduction to my words. I just write, in big block letters—

BECCA IS GOING TO THE PROM BANQUET! FOR REAL!

Then I put the date, May 15, and sign it.

I am excited, but not nearly as out of control as the girls are by Saturday night when we meet in the lounge of the shelter to hem and alter the donated prom dresses. My mother, the rest of the Sisterhood, and Rose are all there to help with the sewing. My mother and I postponed our shopping trip so we could organize our sewing supplies. I'm the seamstress in charge.

The doors to the lounge have been closed and "women only" signs have been put on them.

My mother and I brought a box of thread and the spools in every color of the rainbow. Rose bought fifty sewing needles and Lizabett brought various colors of netting and these little satin roses that can be used for accents. Marilee brought a half-dozen scissors from her office at the Pews and a glossy magazine called *Prom Wear* that she got somewhere.

The dresses have been delivered to Carly's aunt, and Carly is bringing them down to the shelter in Randy's Jeep. She called us on her cell phone ten minutes ago to let us know she'd turned off the freeway and is driving down Melrose.

"The dresses are all tagged," I tell the girls what Carly told me. "So there's no need to rush the dresses when they come in."

We have over forty girls sitting in the lounge, doing nothing but waiting. I've never seen things this quiet. Part of that is because the guys are all supposed to be either in the computer lab or out back playing basketball.

We hear the Jeep pull up outside, and I know the quiet is over. The girls open the lounge door and head for the main door.

"Whoa there," Mark calls out as he comes down the hall from his office.

The girls don't stop, but they slow down enough that they won't trample anyone bringing the dresses inside.

"Thanks for the crowd control," I say to Mark as I start to follow the girls. I feel a lot more comfortable around Mark since we talked last night.

He grins as he follows me. "Law school was good for something. I learned to speak loud enough to be heard over almost anything."

"I'm surprised they didn't get you for badgering your witnesses if that's the way you talked," I say with an answering grin as we reach the open doorway.

He winks at me. "They tried."

Mark stops just inside the door. "I better not get too close to the dresses."

"That's the rules," I say as I step through the door. The setting sun shines in my eyes so I put my hand up for shade.

The girls are lined up beside the white Jeep that is parked on the street right in front of the shelter. Carly has stepped out and is walking around to the back door of the vehicle. The girls are lined up on the sidewalk. The cars buzzing down Melrose Avenue don't have their lights on yet even though they will in a half hour.

I step down the stairs in the front of the shelter and stand in the partial shade from a corner of the building. I fold my arms across my chest. A sudden chill breeze blows in from the west. I've never liked to stand out on the street in front of the shelter. It feels so exposed.

This is not the manicured streets of San Marino or the restored streets of Old Town Pasadena. This section of Melrose is broken down and rough. The tattoo parlor across the street is painted bubble-gum pink and has black bars on its windows. The sidewalks have deep cracks. There are no trees, and the only thing around resembling grass is weeds. Most of the area that should be lawn is just hard dirt. I look back up the stairs and am glad to see that Mark is standing beside the opened door at the top.

"Hey, Candy baby." The shout comes from down the street.

I turn to look. It's that guy Jason who gave me the note for Candice the other day. He's still wearing the same orange T-shirt and cocky grin.

He's bad news. I don't know why I know that. Instinct, I guess. He looks at Candice like he owns her. And he's got what looks like a knife sheath clipped to his boots.

"Who you calling baby?" Candice calls back to Jason.

"You know who," Jason says as he keeps walking toward us.

Candice turns away, but then I see a satisfied smile on her face. She checks to be sure Jason is still coming toward her.

I hear footsteps and turn to see Mark walking down the stairs.

"Remember the rules," Mark says quietly to Candice. "Stick with kids who are clean and sober."

"He doesn't mean anything," Candice mutters to Mark. "He and I just used to hang out. That's all. We're old friends."

Jason stops a few feet from us all and glares at Mark.

"You got a problem with me?" Jason says.

"You're free to walk down the sidewalk," Mark says with a shrug.

I've heard Mark has a reputation for dealing with belligerent kids. With his body language, he doesn't back down, but he doesn't step things up, either.

Jason looks a little confused at Mark's attitude.

Everyone is silent for a minute.

"Who wants to help carry the dresses inside?" Carly asks and suddenly she has everyone's attention, even Candice's.

The girls carefully take the dresses from the Jeep. Candice gives Jason a wave, but she follows the other girls inside. She probably sees what I see—one of the dresses is copper-colored.

Mark goes back to his office and we take all of the dresses into the lounge. We set them on the sofas before we start removing the plastic bags that cover them. I am pleased to see that the dresses are tagged with the girls' names. I knew they would be tagged somehow, but I thought the women might have a numbering system. I am glad they used the girls' names. Things are impersonal enough in their world as it is.

The copper dress is tagged with Candice's name. She twirls around with that dress in her arms and I'm sure she has forgotten all about Jason.

"Hey, look at this," Lupe gives a yell as Carly hands her a dress.

I take one look at the dress Lupe holds and I know Mrs. Russo has kept her promise. She must have purchased this special for Lupe. The material is fire-engine red and looks like satin. It will fit Lupe like a glove.

"I'm going to be hot," Lupe says with satisfaction as she swings the dress around and dances with it like Candice is doing.

It takes a few minutes to get all of the dresses to the right girls. I let the girls enjoy the fantasy of their dresses for a minute. Most of them have never even owned a dress of any kind. And these dresses are made for dreams. There are silk bands and gossamer net. Some dresses are strapless, and some have wraps that are attached. I see one dress that's coral, another that's lavender and one that's sea green. All together they remind me of a kaleidoscope of color and texture. There's smooth shiny satin and soft wispy rayon.

When the girls calm down, we decide to break into groups to make the alterations. We put one experienced seamstress with each group and give everyone a needle and some thread. In fifteen minutes, there is conversation going on around each dress being altered. It all reminds me of the first days of the Sisterhood of the Dropped Stitches. We were just like these girls, reluctant to talk until we started making something.

I feel an urge to get poetic about women sewing and talking throughout the centuries, but I don't. The girls that are paying attention will think of it themselves, and it will mean more to them than if someone tells them.

I look over at my mom. She has her head bowed over a section of sky blue satin, hand-sewing a dart. She would understand about all the women working together. I'm glad we can share this day even if it means postponing shopping for my dress.

I hear a soft knock on the door to the lounge and I get up to answer it.

Mark's there. "I forgot to ask you something earlier."

I step out of the lounge and close the door. "Is it something about the dresses?"

Mark shakes his head. He's looking down at the floor and I've never seen him look so shy. "I have a favor to ask."

"Really?" I can't wait to tell Carly. She'll think this is a good sign. Even I think this is a good sign. First, the chairs pulled together and then a favor.

"Your friend's brother came by to see me yesterday. You know, Quinn."

I nod and grimace. I can tell where this is going. "Sorry. He wanted to check you out when he thought you were going to the banquet with Lizabett—that's all."

"He asked me to visit his church tomorrow," Mark says.

"Oh."

"He said you've been there."

"Once. That's all. It's not like I'm a regular."

"Would you go with me?"

"Ahhh, sure." I say and then I realize I sound uncertain. "Of course."

"Good," Mark says and he sounds relieved. He looks up and smiles. "That's great."

"The pastor is—ah, interesting." I don't know how to warn Mark. "The man seems to know things."

"Well, I'm sure he went to seminary."

"No, I mean things about people." I didn't want to say they are things about me. I want to warn Mark off the pastor, not off of me.

"Shall I pick you up or do you want to meet me somewhere?" he asks.

I'm not sure I'm ready to introduce Mark to my parents. This church thing seems even more serious than the prom banquet. "Maybe we could meet at the church."

"Eleven o'clock. And let's do lunch after."

I nod.

Mark turns around to walk back to his office, but then turns and faces me again. "Thanks. I was hoping you would go with me."

"No problem." I grin.

I slip back into the lounge and, there has been so much talking and sewing, that no one even particularly missed me. I'm glad, because I want to just enjoy this moment for a while. I think I just got asked out on a real date by Mark.

Chapter Eleven

"The artist is a receptacle for emotions that come from all over the place: from the sky, from the earth, from a scrap of paper, from a passing shape…"

—Pablo Picasso

One day the Sisterhood piled all of our yarn onto the table in our room at the Pews. It was a jumble of ivory, garnet, meadow green, sunshine yellow and a dozen shades of blue. That was the day Lizabett brought us the Picasso quote. She said we needed to appreciate the artist hiding in each of us. I told her I didn't have an artist hiding in me, but she disagreed. Everyone could appreciate color she said and she was right.

That night we didn't knit; we just sat and admired the colors we had in our pile. You would have thought we were the great artist himself. I almost wished I could paint a picture of the yarn, especially with our shiny pink knitting needles sticking out like chopsticks. I told Lizabett I would call it "Chinese Woman Hiding in Yarn."

Not that it looked like any kind of a woman particularly, but Lizabett agreed Picasso would have named it that anyway. We all went out for egg rolls after the meeting to celebrate my painting that could have been.

I wake up and think about that old pile of yarn. I'd been thinking about it yesterday, too, before I talked to Mark, when we worked on those dresses. All of those fabric colors reminded me of the yarn and the woman in hiding. And then I think of Picasso and landscapes and beauty. I'm guessing some of the girls will come out of hiding when they wear their dresses and we'll be surprised at their beauty. I hope so, anyway.

I know I'm surprised at myself. I'm going to church on a date, and I'm as excited as if I were going to the best party ever. I'm hoping the day will unfold into something beautiful, like a Picasso painting, which is generally vibrant even if it's coming to a person in odd shapes. My life has lots of those odd shapes lately.

When I get to Pasadena, I go to pick up Lizabett. Her car is still in the shop, and we're planning to surprise Marilee and Carly. Of course, I told Lizabett last night about Mark meeting me at church and I think she's coming just to see the looks on Marilee's and Carly's faces when they see us—and Mark. She told me she can get a ride home with Marilee so I shouldn't worry about even sitting with her in church. She gives me a grin when she says it, and I give her one right back.

I barely get inside the church before my eyes are drawn to the stained-glass window at the side of the church.

Somehow I didn't get a full look at that last Sunday. It's full of vivid colors, and we're into color these days.

Marilee is beaming as she walks toward us. I don't see Carly right now, but Marilee is looking like the sunrise, flushed a little pink and glowing.

"Oh, my," Marilee says when she reaches Lizabett and me. She puts her hands out to us and we each take one. "What a blessed morning."

Now, I could never say anything about a morning being blessed without sounding like an idiot, but it sounds natural coming from Marilee's lips. I think maybe she's the kind of person who can make pronouncements and get away with it. It goes with her earth mother style. Maybe she should look into being a weather person on television. I could see her telling everyone the storm of the century is on its way and making it all sound majestic.

"I'm meeting Mark here," I say because it seems the right thing to do since Marilee is already standing there, looking at us like we're a miracle.

"Seriously?" Marilee squeals.

I nod. "Quinn invited him."

"Wonderful," Marilee says.

"Where's Carly?" Lizabett asks and I know she's searching for distraction like I am. Just being in church makes me nervous.

Marilee turns around. "I think she went outside to see if Randy is here yet. A friend of his is dropping him off."

Lizabett had already told me that Quinn was working today so he won't be here. He tries to arrange his schedule with the fire department to have Sundays off, but sometimes he still needs to work the day.

"Maybe I should go outside and wait for—" I begin and then I see Mark come in the door. I've never seen him in a suit before and I must say he looks good. He glances around the church until he sees me and then he starts walking toward me. I can't even finish the sentence I was speaking to Marilee.

By the time Mark gets to me, the organist has started to play, and Marilee motions us to a seat. Mark waits for the women to file into the pew before him and I see Marilee nod in approval.

"He's a gentleman," she whispers to me as she passes by me.

Finally, we're all seated. Marilee and Lizabett are to my left and Mark is to my right. Carly joins us just before it's time to begin. Apparently, Randy is late so Carly saves him a seat on the end of our row.

Then the pastor starts to talk, and I try to listen. He starts off talking about some leper so I figure I am safe. The pastor's not going to go inside my soul and talk about sensitive issues today. Of course, it's too bad about the poor leper. I wouldn't like to be set aside like he was with no one to talk to. Ooh, and those sores. I don't have to put any effort into having compassion for the poor man when the pastor talks about the sores. I hope the sisters notice and see that my heart is just fine the way it is.

I'm thinking the pastor is going to go with a "be thankful for your health" theme, but he surprises me. The leper gets healed. Well, so much for being worried about health. I hear Lizabett breath a sigh of relief. Even without the open sores, we both know a little about how the leper must have felt because we had cancer.

I think Mark knew what memories the story of leper stirred up in me because he put his hand over mine and gave it a little squeeze.

I heard Lizabett give another little sigh, but I was pretty sure it had nothing to do with cancer or leprosy.

Mark took his hand back, and I'm trying to concentrate in case Mark asks me any questions afterward. I'm working up to feeling really grateful to God that all of us in the Sisterhood are well now, when the pastor says something puzzling.

"Leprosy wasn't even this man's biggest problem," the pastor says in his booming voice. "It wasn't his health that he needed to work on. No, it was the sin in his heart. His selfishness, his vanity, his pettiness. Jesus didn't tell him he'd cure him from his leprosy; he said he'd forgive his sins."

I wouldn't want to say anything, of course, but I'd been sick like the leper had been. If the pastor had asked me, I would have told him the man wanted to be healed a whole lot more than he wanted forgiveness. He could probably live with a few little sins. It's not like he'd murdered anyone. At least, I didn't think so.

And then I looked around me. Marilee was looking intently at the pastor as if she had known what it was to be weighed down with sins. Marilee? She wouldn't hurt a fly. How much of a problem could sin be in her life?

I look at Mark and see he's as puzzled as I am.

I hold my breath. The pastor is beginning to talk about rejection. About being scared. About lying on your bed trying to keep the tears from running down your cheeks. He's got me again. I forget all about the leper. My mind goes back to the dark days when I was small. I can almost feel myself curled up on the side of the bed, squeezing myself as close to the wall as I can. My teeth are clenched so I won't make a sound as I cry. I wish I was invisible to the whole world.

Maybe the pastor is right. There are some things worse than leprosy.

I wish Mark was still holding my hand. I'm not sure I'm the kind of person who should go to church. I don't know how the pastor knows about me, but he does.

After everyone sings a final hymn, Mark slips out the side door with me.

"Well," Mark says. He doesn't look any happier than I am.

I nod. "I don't know what I was thinking to come back here."

"At least no one can say I didn't give it a try," Mark says.

We walk to the parking lot and Mark opens his car door for me. I climb into his car. I left my keys with Lizabett and she's going to drive my car back to the Pews. When Mark gets in the car, I lock the door on my side. He looks at me and then he does the same to his door. We both know we don't need to lock those doors, but we're not going to unlock them all the same.

"How does he know those things about me?" Mark says as he looks straight ahead.

"You? It was me."

"I'm not always proud of what I've done in life. Not that I've done anything that bad. It's just sometimes I can be a real pain."

"You should ask the sisters about me," I say. "They'll tell you I can be a pain, too."

He turns and looks at me. "I guess it's both of us then."

I nod and we sit there for a little bit.

"Do you think we really need Jesus to be happy in life?" Mark finally asks.

"I hope not," I say.

"Yeah, me, too."

We decide to go to the Pews for lunch. I tell Mark that the others might be there too, but he says he's heard so much about the place that he wants to see it.

Mark drives us to Old Town and we begin walking from the parking structure down Colorado Avenue. There are quite a few people on the street for a late Sunday morning. We stop in front of an aroma shop that has a hundred smells inside its walls. The door is open to the street and I can smell lavender. It's dark inside, but I can still see. The candles are arranged in rows of different colors. Pinks, blues, yellows. Picasso could learn a thing or two about organizing his colors from this shop. I decide to come back later.

Uncle Lou is sitting at the counter reading the newspaper when we walk into the Pews. I look at the clock and it's eleven-thirty. We're just a little ahead of the lunch crowd.

Uncle Lou stands up when he sees Mark. "Who have we here?"

"This is Mark. From the shelter," I say.

"Ah." Uncle Lou walks over and holds out his hand. "I've heard you do good things down there."

"Thanks," Mark says as he shakes hands.

Uncle Lou motions us to a table in the back. "I know the others are probably coming, too, so I'm giving you a table for two. I've got plenty of tables. There's no reason for everyone to crowd together. You tell them I said so."

We haven't even gotten our menus when the others come in. Carly and Randy enter first and then Marilee and Lizabett. For a second, I think they're going to pretend that they don't see Mark and me.

But then Marilee walks over. "It was so good to see you both in church. Pastor Engstrom said he'd like to meet the two of you some time. He saw you from the pulpit, but you didn't come by to say hello."

I nod. "Maybe some other time."

I'm hoping my short answer gives Marilee a clue. I don't know about Mark, but I'm not going to shake hands with that man any time soon.

"Maybe we'll get back at Christmas," Mark adds gamely.

Marilee is apparently happy enough with our answers because she joins Lizabett at a table over by the counter. Carly and Randy head over to their own table on the opposite side of the Pews.

"Christmas?" I whisper when Marilee is out of hearing distance. "You shouldn't promise Christmas."

"Well, everybody goes to church at Christmas."

"Not if they're Jewish."

"Oh, yeah." Mark winces. "Sorry about that. I guess I forgot."

"No problem."

"Well, maybe we can go before Christmas then," Mark says.

I don't know what to say to that. He said "we." I don't want to ask if that means he'll be hanging around with me then.

"So tell me about this Sisterhood thing," Mark says. "And about the cancer. That must have been hard."

I don't really intend to tell him much, but when I look at the clock an hour later I realize I've told him everything. He just kept asking questions and I kept talking. We've both eaten our chicken Caesar salads and, by now, Mark knows everything about my cancer and the Sisterhood. I even threw in a few things about law school. And my mother.

"You're a good listener," I tell him. I'll need to let Carly know that it's Mark who has the good ears, not me.

"I wanted to know more about you."

I can feel my face turning a little pink. I'm saved from saying anything foolish in return though because Randy walks over to say goodbye to us.

"I hate to leave," Randy says as he holds out his hand to Mark. "Wanted to say it was good to meet you though. I hope we see you around."

Mark stands up and shakes Randy's hand. "Thanks."

It only takes a few minutes for Randy to leave and Mark follows close behind him. I need to drive my car home and Lizabett left it up in the parking structure for me. Mark says he'll see me tomorrow and I manage to thank him for lunch.

I sit back down at the table after Mark leaves the Pews.

It doesn't take a minute before Marilee, Lizabett and Carly are all crowded around my table.

"Way to go, Becca," Lizabett says as she lifts up her hand to give me a high five.

I high-five her. "It was nothing."

"Nothing?" Carly says. "That was a date if I've ever seen one."

"Yeah," I say and I grin.

"With Mark," Marilee says.

I nod and half expect Marilee to want to say a prayer of thanks or something. She doesn't mention it and I'm oddly disappointed.

"So—" Lizabett says. "Tell us everything."

"Maybe later," I say. I'm not being coy. I'll need to think about our conversation to remember it.

Fortunately, everyone lets me go with that.

Before I know it, we are sitting back in the Sisterhood room and talking about the dresses for the upcoming prom banquet. Some of the girls are putting rows of those tiny satin roses around their waists or the bottoms of their dresses. Lizabett is the one who brought the roses and she says she can get some more at a fabric store she knows about.

"And did you see those shoes Candice has?" Carly says. "I think they're four-inches tall."

"Four and a half," Marilee corrects her. "I measured."

"I hope she knows how to walk in those things," I say. I brought my iced tea back with me, and I take a sip.

"She says she's going to need a man to lean on," Lizabett offers. She has her leftover French fries beside her and she slides the plate toward me.

"So that's her plan," I say. I take a French fry and dip it in some ketchup on the side of the plate. I know I should get all concerned because Candice is trying to maneuver a way to have a date for the prom banquet. I can see her now explaining why she needs a man to walk with her and sit beside her and get punch for her.

"Maybe Mark will ease up on the date thing," Marilee says.

"Don't count on it," I say with a frown. Maybe I should get Candice a cane. That would give her second thoughts. I lift the French fry to my mouth and then lean over to get another one. "He follows the rules."

Everyone is silent for a minute and I finally look up from the fries and notice that everyone is looking at me. "What? Do I have ketchup on my chin?"

"You sound like you don't approve of Mark following the rules," Carly says.

"Well, it is a little inconvenient."

"You always follow the rules," Lizabett says in disbelief. "You've never cared before if they were easy to follow or not. You said rules are rules. They'll save our lives."

"Well, that was different. No one is going to die if they have a date for the prom banquet, whatever it is."

"No one would have died if we'd skipped a day with our vitamins, either," Lizabett says. "But you called us up on the telephone and made us double-swear that we'd taken them."

I look around at my friends. I suppose they have a right to be puzzled.

"Maybe I was wrong," I say. "Maybe we could have loosened up a bit."

Everyone is silent again.

"It's Mark," Carly finally says. "He's gotten to you."

"Gotten to your *heart*," Lizabett adds just in case I have any question about what Carly meant.

"I'm just being practical," I say. "I just think it's better to let the kids have some fun. What can happen anyway? I'm not getting a heart. I'm getting practical."

"And if there's less rules, there's less for the chaperones to do," Marilee adds with a little wiggle of her eyebrows. "That gives you more time with Mark."

"This isn't about me and him. It's about the kids."

We pass the plate of fries around and Lizabett asks me if I have the journal with me. I reach into my purse and pull it out for her.

"Knock yourself out," I say. "Just remember people are going to be reading that, so don't say anything about me and my heart. It sounds silly. I'm just being sensible. And I'm going to leave the shelter any day now."

I take another fry off of the plate.

Hi, this is Lizabett—I just had to write it all down. Becca's got a heart. I just know it. She's sitting here scowling at me, but I know she's worried about her kids having fun. She can't tell me that doesn't mean she's got a heart for them. And that bit about her leaving the shelter—that's all smoke and mirrors. It'll never happen.

She won't want me to say this, but I think she's got a heart for Mark, too. I am so, so glad that Mark's grandmother said that Becca could be his date for this prom banquet. I wouldn't have been able to go on a date with Mark, not knowing how Becca feels about him. I would have felt awful. If you read this, Becca—that's AWFUL. Don't ever ask me to go out with your boyfriend again.

Becca is looking beautiful these days. I think all of this vacation is doing her a world of good. I haven't seen her with that haunted look lately. And, she's not tapping her fingers or her feet or anything. No hiccups, either. She's wearing a turquoise dress today. I'm glad Mark got a chance to see her in turquoise; it brings out the color of her eyes. I know Becca's mother is planning to get a drop-dead gorgeous dress for her to wear to the prom banquet. I would be jealous if it were anyone but Becca. She deserves it.

I'm going to give the journal back to Becca now. Before I do though, I want to say that I always thought she had a heart. It was just buried before like that Chinese woman under the yarn Becca's been talking about. If you're reading this, Becca, I'm sorry if you don't want people to know about your heart. To me, it's beautiful. Anyone can follow rules; it takes someone special to have a heart. You make a beautiful Tin-Man.

Love, Lizabett

Chapter Twelve

"I wasn't satisfied just to earn a good living. I was looking to make a statement."

—Donald J. Trump

The Sisterhood was never about money, but Carly brought us this quote anyway. She wanted us to know that sometimes money was just the beginning for some people. A tool to use in their lives. We listened to her talk, all thinking that she must have a lot of money for it to even be an issue for her. Tools for me were more like fingernail clippers, not trust funds. I wondered if Carly might even know The Donald. It wasn't until later that we realized she was trying to say she didn't have any money. It taught me to not leap to conclusions about what people were trying to say.

This is Becca, and about now I'm wishing that Carly did know The Donald. All of us in the Sisterhood are sitting at our table in the Pews with a big sheet of white paper in front of us. We're making a list of places where we can have the prom banquet. Without money, our prospects are not so good.

"Well, we do have the Pews," Lizabett says for the fifth time in the past half hour.

So far, that's the only name on our list. It's right up there in the top corner of our big piece of paper with all of that white space beneath it.

"This place is too small though," Marilee says. "I'd forgotten that half of our seating is counter seating, and we can't ask people to sit on those stools at the counter for their banquet. That's not very classy."

"A few people can sit in here," I say. We could probably seat eight at the table we have in our Sisterhood room. I look around. We'd have to bring in a few metal folding chairs, but it could be done. The table has some scars on it, but a white tablecloth would cover those.

"Who would want to miss out on all of the fun, sitting back here?" Carly asks.

Carly is the one who hated looking out the French doors from our room into the area where the real diners were. She always felt we were left out of the party sitting back here. And she was right. I liked the quiet here though. And I was taken with the shadows. Because we didn't have a real window in this room, we had lots of shadows. When I think of it, I get uneasy picturing those kids in the shadows though.

"Mark won't let any of the kids sit back here," I say. "It's too private, if you know what I mean."

Carly and Marilee nod.

"If it was warmer out at night, we could have it in the

courtyard of the city hall," Lizabett says. "Remember, we checked that out when we were looking for a place for my class to do their ballet performance. Non-profits can use that space for free."

"It would be too cold, though," I say. "Wouldn't it?"

"Only a few of the girls have wraps for their dresses," Marilee reminds us. "We can't have something outdoors. We'd have to buy everyone coats. It'd cost a fortune."

Which brings us back to money.

"I wish one of us knew The Donald." I say glumly, thinking back to that conversation of years ago. "I don't know how we're going to do this without money. We have more than ninety people coming to this thing, and we need to seat them in comfort."

"Not just seat them. We need to give them a little room to walk around, too," Carly says. "No one wants to be sitting on top of each other."

"Except for Candice," I mutter. It's Monday, and I already had to talk to Candice about appropriate banquet behavior when I was at the shelter earlier. I told her no necking. No lap sitting. No suggestive moving around. "I'm thinking of confiscating those heels of hers. She thinks she's Madonna when she wears them."

"She's young," Marilee says.

"She's trouble. I'm beginning to think we should let the kids have dates just so we don't have all this back and forth as they try to impress each other before the banquet."

"I thought Candice liked some guy named Rick—or is it Ricky?" Lizabett asks. "She talked about him the other night."

"She talks about all of the guys. But maybe Ricky is special to her. He's one of the computer guys, and he helps her with this Web site she has going. It seems real important to her."

"I don't take Candice as the Web site kind of person," Carly says with a frown.

I shrug. "Then maybe it is about spending time with Ricky. They spend hours together in the computer lab."

"Supervised, I hope," Marilee says.

"The kids are always supervised in the computer lab."

"Well, then—" Carly says. "It must be true love."

I notice Lizabett has been drawing little boxes on the big paper while we've been talking.

"Designing us a banquet hall?" I ask Lizabett.

She smiles up. "I wish. Just doodling."

"Have you talked to Mark about the fact that we don't have a place for the banquet?" Marilee asks me.

"No," I say. I don't add that I dread doing that. I told him I would handle the banquet. So far, I haven't gotten it all together.

"You'll need to tell him soon."

"Maybe we could just decorate the lounge at the shelter," Lizabett offers. "That would be big enough."

Now that would make me feel like a total failure. "The kids expect to at least leave the shelter."

"It would eliminate the need for transportation if we had it there," Marilee says half-heartedly.

We all look at each other.

"Maybe they won't mind sitting at the counter here so much," Marilee finally says. "We could move the stools and have it be stand-up dining."

"Don't they do something like that in Paris?" Lizabett asks with forced cheer. "I think I read something about it. Or maybe it was Tokyo."

"We could certainly call it international," Carly says. "I'm sure they stand up and eat every day somewhere in the world."

"I'll talk to Mark," I say. "I need to give him a report anyway."

"At least we have the food taken care of," Lizabett says. "His grandmother saw to that."

"And the girls have dresses and shoes," Carly adds. "I thought we'd never get all the clothes we need."

I don't bother to remind her that the guys still need their tuxedoes. We can't have the girls looking like Italian models and the guys standing around looking like a bunch of Tarzan wanna-bes.

"I don't know if they can eat chicken cordon bleu standing up though," Marilee says. "Maybe we'll need to change the menu to appetizers like glazed meatballs."

I feel myself slump a little more in my chair. There's nothing exotic about meatballs. Even those little quiches aren't very exciting. Nothing on a toothpick makes it, either.

We're all quiet for a few minutes.

"You can tell Mark I'm getting the music together," Lizabett finally says. "The guy who does the music CDs for our ballet class is willing to set up a sound system and play CDs for the kids. He's got a million of them and he can do it anywhere. The shelter. Here. Anywhere."

"Thanks." I nod. I'll be heading back to the shelter in a little bit. Ordinarily, I don't go there twice in a day, but

Mark wasn't there when I was by earlier. It's time I told him that we are having problems getting everything we need for the prom banquet. I hate to admit defeat, but I don't want to disappoint everyone at the last minute.

I guess Mark was right in the beginning. It is too much for us. For me.

"Take the journal with you," Carly suggests. "Remember we're capturing everything."

"I'm not sure I want my failure preserved in stone forever."

"If we can't pull off this banquet, it's not a failure," Marilee says staunchly. "A person only fails if they don't try something."

"Yeah, right." I say. We both know the kids at the shelter won't buy that one. They know what failure is. They've certainly seen enough of it in their young lives already.

I leave shortly after that to start driving back down to the shelter. There doesn't seem to be any point to sitting around the table with the other sisters and staring at that big sheet of white paper. We don't have any options left for a place to have the prom banquet, and we all know it.

I have the journal in my yarn bag sitting on the car seat next to me. I'm still carrying around that old ball of beige yarn in my bag, as well. The scarf I'm knitting from it is all tangled up by now though. It's pretty much a failure, too. My knitting is always bad when I'm worried.

As I move along with the traffic, I start to think. All of this time I thought I was too pessimistic. For the first time, I start to wonder if maybe I'm not pessimistic enough. Maybe life just will never be easy for me. I can only imagine what depths it would have sunk to if I hadn't been adopted. I really do need to thank my parents pretty soon.

By the time I get off the 101 and drive down Melrose Avenue, I'm feeling sour. The broken down area around the shelter doesn't bother me as much as usual. It looks about how I feel.

I park my car on the street since, for once, there's a parking space in front of the shelter. I only plan to stay long enough to give Mark the bad news. I remember that I still have my goodbye letter in my knitting bag. If I didn't feel a person needed to stand by their promises, even the ones they can't keep, I would get the letter out and read it to the girls today. I can't tell them I've broken my promise and then leave at the same time though. I need to stay around so they can blame me for dashing their hopes. Then, after a while, I can pick myself up and leave. By then, they won't care if I do.

The shelter is quiet for a change when I open the front door. I go to Mark's office and see a note taped to his door. He'll be back in fifteen minutes.

Of course, the note does not say when the fifteen minutes started, but I sit down on the bench outside of the lounge anyway. I feel like waiting. I sit there for a minute or two and then pull the journal out of my bag.

Hi, this is me, Becca. Everyone wants me to record the steps in this prom banquet thing I have going, so I'm going to do just that. It was a terrible idea. I don't know what I was thinking. I've gotten us halfway there and I can't get us any further. This thing is going to be lame, lame, lame. And the kids have started to really believe it could happen.

This is the worst.

I'm never going to forget how excited the girls were as they made their alterations on those prom dresses. I hope some of them get to wear their dresses some place real and not just as a costume for some party some time.

I should have seen it all coming. I think I was born under a black star or something, if there even is such a thing. Maybe I was born under a black hole. That feels more right. A pit.

I wouldn't sit here and go on about me, except I'm sure everyone is going to wonder why I had to say I could pull something like this off when I should have known better. I've been thinking about it and I just don't know. I know it was a bad call, but usually I can see those things coming a mile away.

The Sisterhood will probably tell me it was because my heart got in the way, but I know that's nonsense. All I can figure out is that I wanted to do something with my life to make a difference. It wasn't even so much about the girls. It was about me being a hero to the girls.

When we got to talking about the prom, I wanted to rescue us all, myself included. I wonder if the pastor at that church where Marilee goes knows this about me. He sure seems to dig inside my psyche. I don't think I'll go to church there ever again. I'm not sure I can stand it.

Anyway, I hear footsteps coming down the hall. It's probably Mark.

* * *

I finish tucking the journal back into my knitting bag at the same time as Mark turns the corner in the hall.

"Hey, there," Mark says as he walks closer. "Just the person I want to see."

"Really?" I can hear Carly telling me to have some confidence in myself, but I shake off her voice. Now's not the time for that. I'm better off going for the contrite look.

"Lunch was nice," Mark says.

"Thanks again."

Mark is standing in front of me now with a grin on his face. He's wearing gray sweat pants and a black T-shirt. His face is wet and he holds a small towel in his hand. "I took a break to play some ball with the guys. Those guys have some work to do to play like a team, but I keep trying."

There's not much room behind the shelter, but Mark did put up a fence a few months ago and he's been adding a few things for the kids to do. Everyone says the rough basketball court is the best one.

Hopefully, none of the girls play basketball though. They don't need a close-up of Mark. He looks really good with sweat sticking his black T-shirt to his chest and his brown eyes sparkling like he's just won the game.

"I would think the guys would like being part of a team," I say.

Mark grunts as he sits down on the bench next to me. "We've got all kinds of races here. Neighborhoods, too. I know the guys could form gangs in a heartbeat, but teams are still a problem for them."

"I hadn't noticed that they don't get along."

"Oh, they get along." Mark wipes his face with a small towel. "They just don't go out of their way to pull together. You don't see them covering each other's backs. They don't trust each other. What we have in the shelter here is a truce, not a team."

"I never thought of that."

"The girls have been doing better, at least since the dresses." Mark looks at me. "I hear we have some killer shoes in our closets now."

I nod. "The girls do seem pleased with their dresses and shoes."

All of this talk of trust and teams makes me squirm.

I look down at my lap and start counting to three. One. On the count, I'm going to tell him everything. Two.

Mark clears his throat and I look up at him. "I've been meaning to tell you you're brilliant—"

Three. "Huh?"

"Yeah," Mark says. "You're pulling this whole thing together. I think it's great."

"Well, it's not exactly—"

Mark waves my words away. "I know it's not a real prom. But it's real to these kids. I don't know when I've seen everyone so excited."

Okay, so now I need another breath. I think I can still hear the basketball hitting the wall behind the shelter. "We can't do the thing."

Mark frowns. "What do you mean?"

"We don't even have a place to have the banquet. I mean, we have enough money for the food. And we have the clothes for the girls. But—" I realize my voice has been fading, so I square my shoulders and bring it up a notch. "It's my fault. I should have looked into things before I made any promises."

I can't bear to look at Mark so I stare at the wall across the hall from us. His approval has come to mean a lot to me.

"Well, I'm not going to yell at you or anything," Mark says. "You don't need to brace yourself like that."

I glance over at him and relax. He doesn't look mad. "Sorry."

"We're a team," he says, sounding a little offended. "If you're having trouble finding what you need, you need to tell me."

"I'm having trouble finding what we need."

Mark gives me a quick smile. "Cute."

I grin back at him, even though I know he's not exactly calling me cute.

"So, what do we need?" Mark says.

"The big thing is a place to hold the banquet. We're having around ninety people and we want a sit-down dinner. And it should have some charm to it."

"Something like a wraparound balcony?"

"Sure, that'd be cool," I say.

"And maybe one of those crystal chandeliers?"

Okay, so now I think he's kidding with me so I look at him carefully. "And tuxedoes for the guys."

Mark nods. "Of course. The black and white jobs."

"With something besides tennis shoes for them to wear."

Mark nods. "And I think I heard something about some limos."

Okay, so now I know for sure he's kidding. "I didn't think the shelter had a budget for anything like this."

"It doesn't," Mark says as he stands up. "But I do. I've been saving my paychecks from the shelter for two years now. I don't get my trust-fund money until I'm thirty, but I get a partial interest payment that's enough to live on. I can foot the bill for this prom thing. I thought I'd save my paychecks to paint the place, but I think this prom banquet is more important."

Mark starts to walk back to his office and then turns around. "Just don't tell anyone who's paying."

"You're paying?" I say just to be sure I have this straight.

"Hush." Mark looks down the hall both ways. "Tell them you have an anonymous donor. The kids will like a secret."

I see Mark walk into his office and then he comes back out with a credit card in his hand. The card flashes gold at me. "This should get you reservations at the penthouse ballroom in that hotel downtown—the Marquee—you know the one?"

I nod and stand up. Everyone knows the one.

"I'll call a tuxedo rental place and tell them you're coming in with my card. Then you can give directions to the guys. They can each take the bus there."

I nod and fight the urge to sit down again. I never expected our fairy godmother to be wearing sweat pants and flashing a gold card.

"I'll probably have to arrange the limos," Mark says. "I'll call my father's firm. They have a limo company under contract. We might be able to get a deal."

"But this is your own money," I protest when I get breath to say something. I've already taken the card. It doesn't feel any different than my credit cards, but I still hold it as though it might explode in my fingers. "And I'm not a signer on the card."

"Don't worry," Mark says with a shrug as he grins down at me. "I can call my credit-card company and have your name approved. Don't look so shell-shocked. I thought my grandmother would have told you about the trust fund. She dangles that in front of every woman she wants me to date."

"I don't think she exactly wants you to date me."

Mark grins even wider. "Good. I like to pick my own dates."

I think it's stretching things to say Mark picked me for his date, but I'm not arguing. He might not have had many choices when it came to the prom banquet, but he sure had choices about who he invited to go to church with him.

"By the way," he says. "What color is the dress you're wearing to this thing?"

"I don't know yet."

"Oh. Well let me know when you know. I need to get you a corsage."

I must have looked up at him in bewilderment, because he bent down and gave me a quick kiss on the cheek.

"We're going to a prom, remember?" he said softly. "I thought I'd get you a rose or two. It's an old tradition."

I hear lots of footsteps coming down the hall.

"I guess the game's over," Mark says as he steps back from me and looks down the hall.

I walk over to the bench and sit back down. I think sitting down is for the best since my legs are about to go out. A herd of guys trample by me and, in the midst of it, Mark goes back into his office.

I move my bag closer to me and feel for the Sisterhood notebook. I'm not going to write in it right now, but it's reassuring to feel it there all the same. No one in the Sisterhood is going to believe what just happened. I can't believe what just happened.

And then it hits me—I can't tell them. It's supposed to be a secret. I've never had a secret like this from the Sisterhood before. They expect me to tell them everything. In fact, I made a big deal when Carly was holding things back from us not so long ago.

I pat the notebook again even though I don't have a clue how I'm going to tell anyone about our anonymous donor. I certainly can't write about it in the journal.

Chapter Thirteen

"If you obey all the rules, you miss all the fun."
—Katharine Hepburn

I still remember the day Carly brought this quote to the Sisterhood meeting. It was raining outside, and we were all wet and depressed when the meeting started. The diner was busy that night, and Uncle Lou hadn't brought us our tea when Carly read the quote. Fun was the last thing on our minds that night. I think Carly was trying to make a point with the quote that I should ease up with the lectures on what we needed to do to survive, but she didn't say that. She just read Katharine Hepburn's words and said it would be nice to have some fun for a change and not to worry about so many things.

I have no excuses as I face the others in the Sisterhood. We are standing around the counter in the front section of the Pews. It's the middle of the afternoon. Lizabett just came in from her last class, and Carly will start her waitress shift in a few minutes. Marilee interrupted her bookkeeping and came out of her office to hear what I have to say.

"What do you mean you have a place, but you can't tell us about it?" Marilee asks as she leans on the counter. "People have to know where to go."

"Oh, I can tell you about the place," I say. I'm not doing this well. "We're going to have our prom banquet in the penthouse ballroom of that big hotel downtown, the Marquee. This coming Friday night. I just arranged it. Seven to midnight."

There's a moment's silence and then Lizabett gives a long whistle. I didn't know she could do that.

"Are they donating the room?" Carly asks in confusion.

I shake my head.

"You do know they charge?" Carly keeps at it. "My aunt was going to have some fund-raiser there for her garden group and they decided not to go through with it because it was so expensive."

"It's a pretty penny all right," I agree.

The rest of the sisters just look at me.

"We have an anonymous donor," I say when I can't stand their looks any longer. "Sort of a fairy godmother."

I hope Mark never hears that I described him as a fairy godmother. But what does he expect me to tell people?

"Is it Mrs. Russo?" Marilee asks. "I didn't think she'd spring for more than she already has."

I shake my head. "It's someone else."

The sisters all look at each other and then look back at me.

"It's not your mom, is it?" Carly finally says. "I know she'd do anything, but—"

"I'd never let my parents pay for something like this," I say aghast. "They don't have that kind of money."

"Well, who is it then?" Carly persists.

"I promised I wouldn't tell," I say.

I'm changing my mind. Maybe it would be good for Mark to hear me call him a fairy godmother. He should have at least told me I could tell the Sisterhood. He knows how close we are.

We all just stand there for a minute. They're looking at me and I'm looking at them.

"I thought you said we wouldn't have any more secrets," Lizabett finally says softly.

"I can't help this one."

"You always made it sound like the no-secrets thing is one of your rules," Carly says.

"Sometimes rules just can't be kept."

That statement shuts them up, whether because they agree with me or not I don't know. They're probably just stunned.

We stand there for a few more minutes and then Carly says she needs to start working. Marilee says she needs to finish some bookkeeping so she heads back to her office while Carly walks toward the kitchen.

"Maybe I can write some in the journal," Lizabett says when it's just the two of us standing there. "If you don't need to leave right away or anything."

I have my knitting bag with me so I reach inside it and pull out the journal. "I'm going down the street to that fancy soap place and get some lotion. I'll pick the journal up when I get back."

Lizabett nods and takes the journal from me.

Hi, this is Lizabett. Becca just left the Pews, and I'm sitting in the Sisterhood room with the French doors closed tight. I think something is wrong. I should have known that Becca would never accept defeat with this prom banquet thing. All of the kids are counting on her, and she has that dream date of hers with Mark. I know she'd do anything to make this thing really happen.

But she can't have enough money to rent the ballroom at the Marquee. If Carly's aunt and her friends can't afford it, Becca can't, either. Unless she's using her scholarship money from law school.

I'm afraid to even write those words down here. I don't even know how that scholarship stuff works. I would think they'd just pay the school directly, but maybe they don't always. I don't even know if it's stealing if you use the money for something besides tuition.

I hope Becca doesn't go to jail for this. Maybe I should go ask Marilee about this. She would know about money laws.

No, I shouldn't do that. If I told Marilee, she'd have to turn Becca into the authorities. Especially now that Marilee's a Christian. I think I'd better just keep my thoughts to myself and staple these pages together.

Oh, dear, that's not the solution. I'll need to talk Becca out of what she's doing. If anyone knew what she was doing, she'd never get to practice law, not even if she put the money back and said she was sorry.

And she's got her heart set on going into the law.

I look around and can't find a stapler so I'm going to pull a clip out of my hair to keep these pages shut. My hair has so much curl these days that I need a few clips in it just to maintain order. I look at the clip when I get it out of my hair. It's not very big. Maybe I should use all of the clips in my hair.

Oh, no, I see Becca coming into the Pews. She's back already. Knowing her, she'll be in this room in seconds, asking to pick up the journal. She's too responsible to leave the journal floating around overnight.

"Are you all right?" This is Becca and I'm back with my lotion. Something is wrong with Lizabett though. She's sitting at the table in the Sisterhood room and her hair is falling all over her face. She has pretty hair, with a little bit of a copper color, but she always has it tucked in some way so that she looks dainty. She has pixie features and looks like everyone's kid sister. Except for now. Now, she looks like an escapee from Bedlam. I look closer. Make that a guilty escapee from Bedlam.

"Is something up?" I ask her, trying to sound casual.

"No, is something up with you?" she asks right back.

"Me? No."

"Me neither then," Lizabett says.

"Well, good," I say as I walk toward the table and sit down. "If nothing is up with me and nothing is up with you, maybe we could have something to eat before we head home."

"I have money to pay if you're short on cash," Lizabett says.

"Me? No, I'm fine."

"There'd be no shame in being short," Lizabett continues. "The important thing with money is to stay above board. Keep your dealings honest and all that."

"Sure," I say. By now, I notice that the Sisterhood journal has enough metal clips in it to attract a bolt of lightening. I look closer at Lizabett. "Problems?"

"I'm just worried."

I put my elbows on the table. "Maybe I can help. What's wrong?"

Lizabett looks down at the table and mumbles. "I think a friend of mine has stolen some money, and I don't want Marilee to know about it because she might tell, you know, the authorities."

"Well, if someone is stealing, she should tell the police," I say and then it hits me. If it's someone from the diner, it might be one of the waitresses. They're all working so hard. "Unless, of course, she wants to talk to the person first. Maybe they could put the money back."

Lizabett looks up at me and beams. "That's what they should do, isn't it? Just put the money back and no one needs to know."

"I'm not sure it's that easy."

"But maybe they haven't even really taken the money yet," Lizabett says. "Then all they would have to do is not take it and everything would be fine."

"Well, I guess if they haven't taken it yet, there's nothing to report, especially if they change their mind."

Lizabett nods. She looks relieved. "That's the way I figured it."

"Well, good then," I say. "What do you say we split a chicken sandwich?"

"Sounds good to me," Lizabett says. "Let's get fries, too."

"I'll put the order in," I say as I stand up. I think it's just as well Lizabett stays in the room until I can get some hair clips from Carly. We didn't drive any of Uncle Lou's customers away when we had cancer; there's no reason to start now.

When I get home an hour later, I'm glad I ate at the Pews. I already knew my father had to work tonight and my mother is sitting at the kitchen table looking at a huge catalogue of some kind.

"They've got prom dresses in here," my mother says as she holds up the catalogue. "Since we didn't make it shopping the other day, we could order one from here."

I smile as I sit down at the table with her. I'd put off our shopping trip for a second time because I didn't want to explain the prom banquet might not happen. I didn't want to disappoint my mother. But now it looks like I won't have to disappoint her. I'm happy to buy a dress. "What color do you think I should get?"

"You've always looked good in strong pastel colors. Not the washed-out ones, but the ones that have some depth to them. Maybe something with a blue undertone."

I nod. She sounds like she's been thinking about my prom dress for years and maybe she has been. I give her all I've got. "Mark wanted to know the color of my dress so he could get me a matching corsage."

"Really?" My mother starts with a smile and keeps on

going until she's beaming. I see her struggle to keep things casual. "He sounds like a real gentleman."

"I think he is."

I take the catalogue from my mother. "What kind of skirt should I have? Full or straight?"

"Depends on whether you do straps or not on the top. I like a straight skirt with strapless. With your figure, you could do either, though."

My mother and I spend an hour picking out the dresses that we think are the best. Mostly, I just go along with her opinions. My mother has been waiting for this day since she adopted me. I never thought I could give her something worthy of those pink princesses on my wall. I'd wear a gunnysack if it would please her.

When I tell her the prom is next Friday, she decides we'll order two dresses from the catalogue and return the one we like the least.

"Did Mark say what kind of flowers he's planning to get?" she asks. "If he didn't, that's okay."

I can tell she's trying to not be pushy.

"Roses," I say.

My mother sighs and her eyes get soft. "I had roses for my prom. Pale yellow ones. I thought they were so beautiful."

"You never told me you went to your prom." Which is odd now that I think of it. I always thought she hadn't gone to her prom and that's why it was so important to her that I go to mine. But that's not it.

"I didn't want to—" My mother stops and looks at me. "When you couldn't go, I didn't want to make you feel bad."

"It wouldn't have made me feel bad." I put my hand on my mother's shoulder as I stand up. "Want some cocoa?"

"That'd be great."

I walk toward the stove and reach for the pan I use to boil water. "When we drink it, you can tell me all about your prom."

"I don't know what there is to tell."

I turn around and look at her. "You can start with the guy. Was he cute?"

"Well, he wasn't your father," she says a little primly and then she grins. "But he wasn't bad, either."

I put the water on to boil and get us two cups down from the overhead shelf. I'm glad my mother can finally talk to me about her prom. I wonder what other conversations we never had because I was sick.

"And he did give me that beautiful corsage," she adds. "I don't know where he got the money."

Well, at least I know where Mark got the money for my flowers. No big surprise there.

I put the cocoa mix in the cups. "What was your dress like?"

My mother tells me all about her prom and I wish she had told me years ago. Her face glows when she remembers everything. She could have told me these things when I was sick. Even if I couldn't go, I would have been glad that she had been able to go. It would have given us something to share.

"What kind of shoes did you have?" I ask when there's a lull.

That starts my mother off again. She wore flats because

her date was short. "But I wished I'd worn my heels anyway. I would have only been an inch taller than him with them on and the girls in heels just looked so sophisticated."

I nod, remembering Candice. Some things don't change over time.

We finish our cocoa and mark the pages in the catalogue that have the two dresses we've selected. I'm going to call in the morning and order the dresses.

My mother goes to bed, and I sit in the kitchen for a few more minutes. If my dad had been home, I would have been tempted to give them my thank-you speech tonight. But I'm glad I didn't. I'd like to give my mother her princess fantasy before I say thank you. Maybe then I'll feel like I've given her something for all the years and that my thank you will really mean something.

I'd just as soon let neither of them ever know I was scared when I first came to their home. I was so convinced they would send me back.

I certainly would have never believed there was any way we'd be here eighteen years later picking out dresses fit for a princess and drinking cocoa together.

I stand up and turn off the light before walking down the hall to my bedroom. Life continues to surprise me.

Chapter Fourteen

"Those who don't know how to weep with their whole heart don't know how to laugh either."
—Golda Meir

Our counselor, Rose, was the one who brought this quote to an earlier Sisterhood meeting. I was sure she brought it for me, to show me there was a well-respected Jewish woman who knew how to cry. Back then, I didn't know how to explain that it wasn't knowledge I lacked. I knew how to cry, I just couldn't do it. Well, I supposed I could have started to cry, but I felt like I would not be able to stop if I did. So I kept myself under control.

Rose is going to come to our prom banquet. We weren't sure that she would, but once I found out when we were going to have it, I invited her and she said she'd love to come. Which is wonderful enough, but the really big news is that we think Rose and Uncle Lou are going to come together. I had invited him, as well, of course, and

Marilee just told us that she thinks her uncle has invited Rose to go as his date.

We never thought either one of them dated, so all of the Sisterhood is sitting in our room trying to get a handle on this. Is it good? Is it bad? We don't know.

"Of course, they've dated other people before," Marilee says like she's trying to convince herself it all doesn't mean anything. "It was a long time ago maybe, but—"

"They probably just feel awkward since all the other adults are going as couples," Carly says. "Maybe they just want to blend in."

"Uncle Lou is planning to wear a plaid bow tie," Marilee says. "I don't think he cares about blending in."

"Besides, none of the kids have dates," Lizabett pipes up. "So most people aren't going to be in couples. At least, the kids aren't supposed to pair off, are they?"

"No," I say.

"I guess Randy is my date," Carly says. "But we're going to be so busy catering that night that it won't make any difference."

"It was nice of Mrs. Russo to pay enough to cover the catering," Lizabett says as she looks at Carly anxiously. "She did pay enough, didn't she?"

"With a little left over," Carly says.

Lizabett brightens. "Is that going toward the rent of the ballroom?"

"I don't think so."

"It's going to some of the tux rentals," I say. I don't know why Lizabett is so worried about money lately. I think she's just hoping I'll slip up and tell her who is paying for the ballroom. There's not much chance of that happening.

Lizabett is still frowning so I try to think of something that will distract her from the money.

"Did you finish up what you wanted to write in the journal?" I ask her. "I didn't read what you wrote last night. Not that I could have, I suppose, with all the clips."

I smile to show I'm teasing.

"We're allowed to keep some parts private." Lizabett bristles a little, but she still reaches for the journal when I slide it over toward her.

"Knock yourself out," I say as Lizabett takes the notebook.

Lizabett gets up and goes into the main part of the Pews. I figure she'll sit at a table in there while she writes.

"Aren't you supposed to be journaling?" Marilee says to me with a frown. "Have you put anything in the journal?"

"Of course, I've put things in there. And some of it's personal."

"Well, okay, then," Marilee says with a small smile. "I'll look forward to reading it after the prom banquet."

"Maybe I'll put the recipe in there for the chicken cordon bleu," Carly says. "Randy had to multiply everything to make enough to feed the crowd we have coming. All of that hard work deserves to be documented. I'm glad we got a place like the Marquee to work with though. They're taking care of the tables and everything—even the waiters. All we have to do is show up with the food."

"Hmm, that's unusual," Marilee says. "Did they say why they didn't insist on catering it themselves?"

Carly shrugged. "Whoever's paying for the place made the arrangements. And the hotel is happy. Money talks."

Marilee looks at me. "Sounds like your fairy god-mother has been busy."

"It's not *my* fairy godmother," I correct her. "It's for the kids."

Marilee puts her hands up. "Trust me, I'm not complaining. Generosity is good for the soul. Even for a fairy godmother."

I look out the French doors and see Lizabett sitting at a table, scrunched over the journal and scribbling fiercely.

Hi, this is Lizabett. I started chewing my fingernails again. I don't think I can take a life of crime. Not that it's even my crime. But Becca is one cool cucumber. I can't figure her out. She doesn't look like someone who has just misused her scholarship funds.

I'm thinking maybe it's not the scholarship money. Maybe Becca had some secret stash of money that she's using. Like maybe her real mother isn't dead and sent her a huge check because of feeling so guilty about giving Becca away all those years ago. It could happen. I know my mother would have felt guilty about giving one of her kids away. And I'm sure, with all of my brothers, that she faced that temptation a time or two.

I just looked back into the Sisterhood room and saw Becca looking out at me. I'm going to surprise her. I'm not going to clip these pages back. That's because, Becca, if you're reading this, remember there's still time to call the whole thing off. Don't spend any money that isn't yours to spend. And, if you are spending your own money, think about it.

Remember, the Sisterhood can get through anything together. We're there for you. Love, Lizabett

Lizabett comes back into the room with the journal and marches right over to me. "You can read this if you want, Becca."

I nod as I take the journal she's handing to me. "I will when I get a minute."

"Good," Lizabett says. "It's about the prom banquet. Something you should think about."

I'm not quite so enthusiastic in my nod this time. "Does it have something to do with the corsage Mark is getting me?"

"Mark's getting you a corsage?" Carly squeals. "Since when is he getting you a corsage?"

"Since he asked me, I think. I'm wondering if he's got a package theme going though."

"And that's bad because?" Carly looks at me like I'm crazy.

"I don't want to be an example."

There I've said it. I was lying awake last night, thinking about how nice it was that my mom and I were going to have our princess moment when I realized that I'm probably nothing more than an instructional aid to Mark. Maybe he just picked me at random to go to church with him. Maybe he isn't making a special effort for me. I can just picture him at the shelter telling the guys the steps they need to take so the girls all have a good time at this prom banquet. I bet every girl gets a corsage to match her dress.

I guess I don't mind so much for myself. This prom thing with Mark was always going to be a half-chaperone obligation. But I think my mother will be disappointed if she finds out my prom banquet date was mostly a lesson to some kids.

"What's in the journal has nothing to do with flowers," Lizabett says firmly. "It's just my thoughts."

Lizabett has a funny look on her face.

"You're not feeling bad because you don't have a date, are you?" I ask her. "Because I swear I'll talk to you a lot when we're there. It's not like people are going to be paired off even if they do come together."

"That's true," Marilee says. "We're going to be eating at tables with other people."

"Eight to a table," I say. "You'll have plenty of conversation."

"I'm not worried about a date," Lizabett mumbles.

"Well, you have that cute dress to wear," Marilee says. "I don't know what else you need to worry about."

"Yeah," Carly adds. "We'll all be there."

I sit there listening to Carly and inside I'm agreeing. No matter what happens, the Sisterhood will be there for each other. I know we told ourselves that a lot when we all had cancer, but it's just as true now that we're facing different problems. I'm not sure I've always appreciated that fact as much as I should have. After I thank my parents for all that they've done for me, I need to thank the Sisterhood, as well.

I take the Sisterhood journal home with me that night, but I don't open it up. I know I need to write in it, but I'm tired. I have so much to do before the prom banquet is here. If I get a good night's sleep, I can start in fresh tomorrow. There's only three more days until the prom banquet and there's a lot to do.

The three days go by so fast I can hardly believe it when Friday is here again. I just finished arranging the floral bouquets for the tables yesterday. The hotel had these fantastic old silver candelabras with a place for flowers in the middle and they said we could use them. I know Mark wouldn't mind if I just asked the hotel to do the whole arrangements, but he's already spent so much money and, if I do the flowers, we at least get the arrangements for free so I went to the Flower Mart downtown in the early morning and bought dozens of spring flowers.

I took the flowers to the ballroom this afternoon. The hotel staff had already set the tables up and they were setting chairs around when I got off the elevator. The whole scene almost takes my breath away.

The candelabras are in the middle of the tables which also have formal white cloths covering them. And then there are underskirts of different shades of pink peeking out from under the main table cloth. The chairs have brass arms and the hotel staff is rubbing them down so they shine. What looks like real silver forks and spoons are resting on the table, waiting for someone to put them by the eight place settings each table is going to have.

I walk closer to the tables and then I see them—dainty little glass fingerbowls, one for each place. Mark remembered what I'd told him about Candice's wish. I keep looking around. The girls are going to love this.

There are floor-to-ceiling windows on the left side of the room and sliding-glass doors open out to a terrace that overlooks the city. There are benches for sitting out there and a few trees sitting in pots. I notice a telescope in one corner of the terrace and smile, thinking how excited the kids will be if they can look up at the stars after we eat.

I put flowers in the bowl of each candelabra and leave the room. Mark is going to pick me up at my place at six-thirty and I want to have plenty of time to spend with my mother as I get ready.

I probably should write in the journal a little, since I haven't taken time to look at it since Lizabett wrote a couple of days ago. I keep telling myself that once the prom banquet is over, I will spend a whole afternoon writing everything out so the record will be complete.

My mother is ready for me when I get home. A florist has delivered my corsage and it's in the refrigerator.

"It's beautiful," my mother says as I walk in the door of the house. "He got it from that expensive florist in Beverly Hills. It came with an extra bouquet of flowers, too."

The bouquet is sitting in the middle of the kitchen table as I walk down the hall. There have to be a dozen roses banded together to form a tight-knit top circle set in a glass bowl of sorts. The roses are every color imaginable, red, lavender, coral, cream and yellow.

I'm stunned. Why did he do this?

"The corsage roses are just one color. Pink," my mother says. "They're from the same florist, of course."

I nod. "Maybe he got a package deal?"

"I don't think that florist ever has package deals," my mother says. "Your young man knows his flowers."

My young man is going to get me in trouble here if he's not careful.

"Mark just likes to do things right," I say to my mother. "I wouldn't read too much into it."

I can see my mother's eyes dim.

"I thought you liked him," she says.

"He just needs a date for the prom banquet tonight."

"Well." My mother lifts her head and smiles bravely. "That's a start."

I nod.

"You'll be so beautiful tonight, you'll make his head spin," my mother says.

I grin. "I have no objection to that."

"Good," my mother says as she starts down the hall. "Because I have a bath to start for you. You'll soak in dried rose petals for twenty minutes and then add some French oil to the water. I saw how to do it in this magazine. It's supposed to make your skin glow."

I had already tried on the two dresses we'd ordered and my mother and I both liked the one made out of a deep navy satin the best. It had a square neckline and my mother insisted I borrow her small diamond necklace to wear.

I had picked up a boutonniere on the way home for Mark's tuxedo. It was a single deep red rose. I put it in the refrigerator next to my corsage.

The rose water was relaxing and my mother had left a CD player in the bathroom with one of those relaxing disks. By the time I was ready for the oil part of my bath, I had forgotten every worry I'd ever had about tonight.

Of course, most of my worries had left when I'd seen

the hotel staff in action. They all looked like they knew exactly what to do to make this a wonderful evening for the kids. I'd talked to Carly this morning, and she'd said the hotel kitchen was working with them on the catering, too, so that it was all going to go smoother than she'd even hoped.

Carly told me she'd tried to find out from the hotel staff the name of the benefactor of the evening, but they either didn't know or wouldn't tell her. I was a little disappointed at that. If someone else told what Mark had done, I wouldn't need to keep it a secret from anyone who already knew.

I closed my eyes for a minute. This all felt so good.

Chapter Fifteen

"Joy is very infectious; therefore, be always full of joy."

—Mother Teresa

It was Marilee who brought the Sisterhood this quote. The night she read it to us, we went around the room and told each other about one joyful moment in our life. Carly remembered waving to her mother from the Rose Queen float in the Rose Parade, Lizabett remembered her first ballet lesson, Marilee told us about hitting her first home run. It took me a while to think of a joyful time, but I finally remembered the moment I heard I was going to be adopted. In those first few minutes, I thought all of my sadness would be gone forever. It wasn't until later that I became afraid I wouldn't measure up.

This is Becca and I can't breathe. I think I might be on the edge of one of those joyful moments again. I am standing at the door and I think I see tiny pieces of shiny gold confetti falling down on me. I look again and realize it's just the porch light reflecting on my mother's new brass wind chimes. Mark has rung the doorbell and I just opened the door. Once I see past the confetti, I am still stunned. It is getting dark outside and there are shadows on the porch, but there is Mark in his tuxedo, and behind him, at the curb of my parents' house, is a long white limo with its driver standing there with the door to the limo open.

I could be Oprah. Or the Queen.

I think I'm going to die.

And then I notice something is wrong with Mark's face. I step outside onto the porch. "What happened?"

"The driver told me no one would notice," Mark says as his hand goes to a red bruise on his left cheek.

"The *driver* did that?"

Mark shakes his head. "I had a little disagreement with Jason when we left the shelter."

"But you always talk your way out of trouble," I say as I reach for his hand. Mark is not nearly as heart-stoppingly unbelievable now that I know his cheek is sore. It's nice to have him back to normal. Or me back to normal. Whichever. "Come inside. My mother will know how to get that swelling down."

"I was hoping it would go away on the ride over here," Mark says as we walk into the living room.

My mother, bless her heart, has been upstairs. I know she was trying to be invisible, but she had also staked out the one place in the house where she'd have the best view of our walkway. I'm glad the limousine driver has been standing at attention.

"Mom, we need your help," I call out.

Sure enough, she's there before I get all of the words out.

"Mark had a problem with one of the boys," I say as my mother leads us into the kitchen. Then it occurs to me. "What was Jason doing there?"

"I think Candice invited him by to see her get into the limo," Mark says as he sits down in a kitchen chair and my mom goes to the refrigerator. The kids have gone in their own limousines. "It kind of backfired though. Jason didn't want Candice to go with us, and she didn't like that."

I look at him. "Was she with Ricky?"

"It could have looked like that to Jason even though I told him we weren't allowing dates."

"I'll wager Candice told him differently," I say as I automatically take what my mother gives to me.

Then I look down at what I'm holding in my hands. "Frozen peas?"

My mother nods. "It'll make the swelling go down. Just hold the bag on Mark's cheek until you get where you're going."

"I can do that," Mark says as he reaches his hand out for the package of peas.

"It's better to have someone else hold it," my mother says calmly. "That way it's sure to be on the bruise."

My mother can't even look us in the eye when she says that. She's making it up, of course. Instead, she turns back to the refrigerator and pulls out the corsage Mark sent for me and the boutonniere I got for him. "We can't forget these."

I keep waiting for Mark to say my mother is completely wrong about who should hold the frozen vegetables on a bruise, but he doesn't. Instead, he pins the corsage to my dress like the gentleman he is.

"You look beautiful," Mark says as he stands back to admire the corsage. Well, I guess he's not looking at the corsage when he says it. He's looking me straight in the eye and I think I'm seeing those confetti things again. All I can think about is that, here I am on the most romantic night of my life and I'm holding a bag of frozen peas in my hands. Plus, I can't speak because I feel a hiccup forming in my throat.

My mother must see I'm in trouble. She turns to Mark. "You look very nice, too."

Yes, that's what I would have said.

"The tuxedo is nice," I manage to say in a rush before the hiccup forms. I know what works with my hiccups so I stop breathing.

"Thanks," Mark says with a grin as he holds his elbow out to me. "We should be going or we'll be late."

I nod and keep swallowing back the hiccup. I've never felt like a princess before, but all I have to do is look up at the light in my mother's eyes and I know that I look every glittering bit of the fantasy. Except for the blue tinge to my face, of course, which must be there now that I'm holding my breath.

"It was nice to meet you, Mrs. Snyder," Mark says as we start walking toward the door.

I grab my purse off the table by the front door. My mother wanted me to take a small beaded purse she has, but it is too small. Instead, I have a blue velvet bag that has room for my cell phone and the Sisterhood journal. I know no one will be writing in the journal tonight because we'll all be too busy. But it seems right to take it along anyway. This is a big night for all of us. The journal deserves to be there.

My mother nods and beams at Mark as we walk out of the house.

I have never ridden in a limousine before and I will never forget the feel of the leather seats and the smell of luxury. I slowly start to breathe again and I don't feel a hiccup anywhere inside me. Now this, I think, is what a limousine can do for someone.

I bless my mother and her peas because I am practically required to sit close to Mark so I can tend his bruise. Florence Nightingale would have done the same. I like sitting close in the dark comfort of the limousine. We'd made arrangements to swing by and pick up Marilee and Quinn so we do that. Marilee has never ridden in a limousine before, either. Marilee looks excited even before she sees how close I am sitting to Mark. Then she really looks curious. I open my mouth to explain why Mark and I are so cozy and then I close it again.

Mark escorts me up to the ballroom.

We open the door, and I expect to be feeling the happiness. The chandeliers hang low, their crystals reflecting the light all over the room. The tables are covered with those formal white cloths and there are long sparkling pearlescent streamers hanging from the ceiling to show it's a party.

"It's like being inside a prism," I whisper to Marilee, who is standing on the side next to me. "It's beautiful."

"Something's wrong," Mark says quietly from my other side.

And then I notice it. The happy feeling isn't surrounding me like it should be. The kids are all standing around and they're talking in low voices. Usually, there would be a few whoops and laughs with every heartbeat. We would have certainly heard them as we walked from the elevator to the ballroom entrance. There are almost ninety kids in here. If I didn't know better, I would say they were at a funeral. And that someone had a video camera and was taping them in their grief so they were frozen in it.

They all look okay at first glance. The girls have dresses in apricot, mauve, cream and so many other colors. No one is swirling though. When we tried the dresses on back at the shelter, the girls couldn't stop twirling around. Now, their shoulders are all hunched and there's no joy on their faces. They're not even looking down to admire their shoes. And I know they have some killer shoes.

The guys are no better. They are all wearing tuxedoes, but they don't look comfortable. None of them look like they want to be here.

Candice is the first one to spot us and she runs over to us, kicking off her bronze high heels on the way.

"I'm so sorry," she wails as she stands in front of us. "I never meant for anyone to get hurt."

Tears are streaming down her face and I can sense that Candice is ready to throw herself into someone's arms for comfort. I move a little to give Marilee room to catch her. Marilee was in Candice's sewing group and there's no more sympathetic person in the world than Marilee.

To my surprise, Candice launches herself at me instead. I open my arms because there's nothing else to do. I'm five inches shorter than Candice, but that doesn't stop her from finding my shoulder.

"There, there," I say as I give Candice an awkward pat. "You didn't mean to cause any trouble, did you?"

Candice shakes her head against my shoulder.

I hold Candice for a minute, before Mark clears his throat and she looks up at him.

"I hope you tell Jason that you're sorry, too," Mark says. "His bruise hurts just as bad as mine."

"You hit Jason." I turn to Mark in surprise. "I know he hit you, but I thought you believed in talking and not hitting."

"Jason wasn't very interested in talking."

I hear a surge in the voices in the middle of the room and look up to see that the rest of the kids know that we're here now that Candice has made so much noise

"Hey, man, way to go tonight," one of the guys says as he comes up and thumps Mark on the back. "That Jason needed some taking down. You're a good man for doing it."

"Fighting is never the answer," Mark says, but the boys keep coming to congratulate him. "And, we'll—"

"I know, we'll talk about it in the next group meeting," the first guy says before giving Mark a wicked grin. "But you got him!"

I'm glad Mark left the frozen peas in the car. Somehow, they wouldn't go with the kids' hero worship.

Mark starts to talk about why it's important to resolve differences peacefully and most of the kids take that as their cue to wander back to the middle of the room where they'd been standing before. They still aren't joking around though like I'd expect.

A crew of waiters in tuxedoes comes through the door leading from the kitchen and they line up on the left side of the room. They wear their tuxedoes like uniforms, pressed and proud. The waiters stand military straight.

"Would you look at that," Lupe says. She is one of the few kids who stayed behind and she's moved up to my right. I turn a little so I can see her staring at the waiters as she talks. "They look like a football team. Only fancier."

All of the kids seem as struck by the waiters as Lupe does and it's silent for a minute.

"Well, look at you!" I finally say. I'd been with Lupe for her dentist appointment so I knew the temporary tooth the dentist had put in her mouth made her look better than usual. I hadn't seen her wearing her long red dress, though, and it's stunning.

Lupe twirls around so I can admire her and then she pulls her dress up a little so I can also see the red high heels she's wearing. She whispers, "Look what Mrs. Russo bought for me."

I'd never seen Lupe so happy. "They're gorgeous."

"Do you think I should wear them when I go to my job interviews next month?" she says in a low voice.

"No," I say. "These kind of shoes you save for special occasions."

"I guess," she says.

Once we finish talking about her shoes, Lupe turns to stare some more at the waiters.

"How many waiters did you get?" I turn to Mark and whisper.

He's frowning a little. "Thirty-two. The hotel here uses a three-to-one ratio for guests to waiters."

"Why?"

Mark shrugs. "Rich people don't like to wait for their water refills."

All of a sudden my purse is ringing. I look down at it. "I don't know who would call me here."

Everyone seems to be watching the waiters so I take a step back to answer my phone in peace. In the time it takes me to assure Mrs. Russo that Mark is fine and that the fight was nothing much despite what the police scanner told her, the boys have managed to line up across from the waiters.

"Don't worry," I tell Mrs. Russo. "Everything will be fine."

We say goodbye and I quietly walk back to where Mark stands.

He's watching the kids so I look at them, too.

"What have they got against the waiters?" I ask

"They look military, standing that way, in those tuxedoes."

The guys from the shelter have lined up so they're facing the waiters.

I wonder what the waiters are thinking as the guys take their measure. The waiters must be well-trained because they don't even flinch.

"I can't believe the guys wait until now to become a team," Mark says as he steps forward.

Mark walks straight ahead until he's between the waiters and the shelter guys.

"Why don't we all tell each other our names," Mark says to the waiter that is first in line. "You guys first and then we'll tell you who we are."

"You want to know our *names?*" the waiter asks.

Mark nods. "First and last would be great. And then maybe your favorite basketball team."

The waiters oblige and then the guys from the shelter do the same. By the time the introductions are over, everyone is talking about sports and the tension in the room goes away.

The conversation gets a little bit louder and then a gong sounds for everyone to sit down at the tables. Carly and Randy step out of the kitchen and Lizabett is with them. I give them all a little wave.

Several of the waiters go into the kitchen and push out huge carts of food.

Mark had arranged for a chaperones table so I save a place for Lizabett on one side of me and Mark sits on the other. I figure that sitting with Lizabett is the least Mark and I can do since she could have been Mark's date if she'd wanted to be. Marilee and Quinn sit across the table from us. The other two couples at our table are Carly and Randy, who will join us in a few minutes, and Uncle Lou and our counselor, Rose, who just arrived.

"I'm glad you set the tables up this way," I whisper to Mark.

Mark shrugs. "I figure none of the kids want the chaperones to be sitting at their table." Then he looks at me. "Besides, we need to have a life, too."

Just then a waiter sets a salad plate in front of me.

There's lettuce, little tomatoes, gorgonzola cheese, pears and pine nuts. I can hear the ripple of consternation as the salads are delivered.

"We didn't tell them about pine nuts," I whisper to Mark.

"They'll figure it out," he says. "That's why this is a life experience."

When everyone at the table has a salad plate, I notice that Marilee and Quinn silently bow their heads. Then Carly and Randy, who've just sat down, do the same. Mark looks at me.

"All of them?" he whispers.

I nod.

"Wow."

The rest of the meal is wonderful. Randy had made the chicken cordon bleu just like Candice had seen it prepared on television. I heard her squeal when she saw her plate with it on. I know she's seen the finger bowls, as well, because I see the guys at the table next to us dip their fingers in them and fling the water across their table.

Mark rolls his eyes at me, but he doesn't say anything.

Lizabett has finished her dinner and she asks me if she can write a little bit in the journal. I tell her yes and bring the journal out, but just then the flaming desserts are wheeled out from the kitchen. I know Lizabett will be too busy for the next little while to write anything.

Hi, this is Lizabett. The banquet is over, even those desserts that were so good. One was flaming bananas foster, just like they have in New Orleans. And they had a flaming baked Alaska, too. Everyone is full and happy now.

Mark and Becca are out on the terrace looking through the telescope. Mark has his arm around Becca and I want to say here that I knew they would be a good couple. I finally figured out that Mark is the fairy godmother. With a grandmother like Mrs. Russo, he has to have money of his own. I think Mark really likes our Becca. At least, the look in his eyes says he does. And she makes him laugh.

I don't know what to make of Uncle Lou and our Rose. They've gone out to the terrace, too, and they are standing together and talking in a corner by this fichus tree. At one point, they were waiting in the line to look through the telescope, but then they let the line pass them by and just are standing there talking.

Becca and Mark are coming back into the ballroom now so I'm going to finish up this entry in the journal. I just wanted to mark the night. I think Becca might almost be in love. I've never seen her look at a guy like she's looking at Mark. She's not going to be able to tell us again that she doesn't have a heart. It's showing on her face.

Becca, if you read this, don't be mad. You know it's true.

Love, Lizabett

Chapter Sixteen

"A kiss is a lovely trick designed by nature to stop speech when words become superfluous."

—Ingrid Bergman

Lizabett brought this quote, and other kissing quotes, to us when Marilee was mourning the loss of her "grill man." Marilee had a crush on him before she had cancer and she thought she'd never love again. Which wasn't as dramatic as it sounds, because none of us thought we'd love again. We had our cancer to think about; we had no time for romance.

One of the hard things about spending so many years fighting to be well is that we missed out on the usual teenage things like first kisses and proms. Carly was the only one of us who had gone to her high-school prom and that was because she was older than we were when she was diagnosed. The rest of us never thought we'd go to a prom.

This is Becca and I've been kissed. *Really* kissed, not a peck on the forehead. I'm standing inside my house, leaning against the door I just closed, unable to move. Mark kissed me on the lips when he said good night. It happened so fast I didn't even have to worry about hiccups.

I can't believe it. He really kissed me. I was all prepared for a handshake or another kiss on the forehead. I mean, I knew he'd been pressured into this date by his grandmother. I didn't expect a real genuine kiss.

Oh, my, it was magnificent. His lips pressed against mine and he wasn't in any hurry to end it all.

I wonder what it means.

I'm still standing here leaning against the door when I hear my mother coming down the stairs in her slippers.

"How was it?" my mother says. She's got her robe cinched around her waist and her hair clipped back from her face.

"Wonderful."

"Good. I'll make some hot cocoa and you can tell me all about it."

I lean against the door for a minute or two more. I can't remember if I kissed Mark back. I was kind of surprised. I hope he knows I meant to kiss him back. I start to walk to the kitchen. I kick my high heels off at the hallway leading down to my room.

I sit down at the table before it hits me. "I have law school. I can't be kissing guys."

"He kissed you?" My mother is beaming.

I set my purse down on the table beside me. "Yes, but

I shouldn't have kissed him back. Not that I'm sure I did, but, well—you know—"

"Well, I'm sure if he kissed you, that you kissed him back. That's the way it usually works."

"Do you think so?"

"Absolutely. Now, tell me about the prom banquet. Were the kids excited? Did Lupe like her new dress?" My mother slides a cup of cocoa across the table to me.

I curl my fingers around the warm cup. "Lupe loved her dress. She'll wear it every day if we don't stop her. But the banquet wasn't what I thought it would be. I thought the kids were all excited and then when they got there—" I shrug. "I guess it was more exciting to think about going than to actually go for them."

My mother nods. "Sometimes when you want something a lot, you build up all of these expectations in your mind and then when you see the real thing, you just don't know what to do. You're not disappointed exactly. It's just not what you thought it would be."

I let my mother's words settle. I grip my cocoa cup tighter. I have wanted to ask my mother about my adoption all of my years in this house. I don't know what gives me the courage to do it tonight, but I start. "Is that the way you felt when you adopted me?"

"Goodness, what are you talking about?"

"When you adopted me," I struggle on. "I know you and Dad had expectations. And I wasn't the little girl you thought I would be, but—"

"Of course you were the little girl we thought you would be. We specifically asked for a girl."

"But you wanted a princess girl. I'm more of a—

well—I've told the Sisterhood I'm a little like the Tin Man, you know, the one with no heart."

"Oh, Becca." My mother gets up from her chair and walks over to me. She puts her arm around my shoulders. "You've always had a heart. A mother just needs to look into your eyes to know that."

"I didn't like the princesses much though," I mutter against the terry cloth of her robe.

My mother steps back and looks at me. "What princesses?"

"The ones on my wallpaper."

"Your father got that wallpaper on sale. We didn't know what to get for your room. We thought about waiting and decorating it together, but the counselors advised us to have the room all ready for you. We thought you liked those princesses. And you never said anything."

"So you don't care about those pink princesses?"

My mother shakes her head. "Not one little bit."

"Really?"

"Really." My mother walks back to her chair. "Now, tell me about this kiss."

I sit there drinking cocoa with my mother and telling her all about the evening. I tell her about all of the kids and the flaming desserts then I tell her about the telescope that looks out into the stars.

"It was Mark's telescope," I say. "He brought it to the hotel so the kids could see through it. He likes to watch the night sky and the hotel terrace was high enough that we were above the city lights so we could see better. I think everybody liked looking at the stars."

"He sounds like quite the guy," my mother says. "Stars and a kiss."

I grin. "He is. Not that it matters since I'm going to be too busy with law school to see too much of him." I have to keep telling myself that. Maybe I'll eventually believe it.

I can see my mother set to protest when my cell phone rings. For a split second, I think it's Mark calling to say good night. I know it can't be him though because he has to get all of the kids settled down first. He probably only got back to the shelter a few minutes ago.

"Hello," I answer.

"Becca, is that you?"

I have to strain to hear the voice. "Mrs. Russo?"

"Mark's been hurt. There was a knife fight and the police are sending him to the hospital. Oh, Becca, you have to go see what's wrong."

I pull the journal out of my purse, as well. I need something to write on. "What hospital? Are you sure it's Mark? Did the police call you?"

"I heard it on my scanner and they didn't mention names, of course, but it's at the shelter address and I know it's him. Please, Becca, you have to help me. He could be dying."

I have the pencil all poised to write down the hospital name, but there is no name and I realize my hand is shaking too badly to write anything anyway. I assure Mrs. Russo I will do what I can to find out more and we hang up.

"Oh, Mom," I say as I look up. "That's Mrs. Russo—she heard something on her police scanner and she's convinced Mark's hurt and in some hospital now. And I don't even know if it's true or which hospital it might be."

"We'll have to figure it out then. Didn't you say Marilee is dating a fireman? I bet he'd know how to figure out what happened."

I feel better all ready. I'll call the Sisterhood. Together, we can figure anything out.

It takes me five minutes to call each of the sisters. I call Marilee first so she can call Quinn. Then I call Carly and Lizabett. They're all getting ready to come with me if Mark is hurt. Carly says she'll start out to Lizabett's and stay there until I call so that she can bring Lizabett with her if we need to go to a hospital. Marilee tells me she'll call her church prayer chain while she waits for Quinn to find out something.

Quinn is the one who calls me back. "They've taken him to Good Samaritan Hospital."

"It is Mark? Is it bad?"

Quinn hesitates. "Yes, it's Mark. My police contact told me he took a knife to the chest. I don't know more than that. Apparently, there was some fight earlier and the guy came back."

"Jason."

"Nobody mentioned the attacker's name. Look, Marilee and I will meet you at the hospital. He's in the emergency room now. And we'll be praying."

"Thanks."

I barely have time to call Mrs. Russo back and tell her which hospital Mark is in before my mother comes back down the stairs.

"Let me drive you," my mother says.

I nod and grab my purse, slipping the journal into it as I follow my mother toward the door.

* * *

I am tapping my fingers against the wooden arms of the chairs in the emergency room. They're old chairs and the upholstery has been cleaned until it's faded. Why do emergency rooms always have that smell to them, like there's some bad odor trying to break through the disinfectant but it just can't quite make it?

Mrs. Russo came into the emergency room shortly after my mother and I did so we're all sitting together. I'm glad my mother is here to talk to Mrs. Russo because I can't seem to put together a coherent sentence. The nurses told Mrs. Russo more than they would tell me so I know Mark is in surgery and they're trying to repair the knife wound.

All of the sisters are on their way to the hospital, but they haven't arrived yet. Marilee even asked if their pastor could come by, and I said yes. I knew we needed help and he was already in the hospital waiting with someone else who was in surgery.

Mrs. Russo's skin is pale and she's not wearing any makeup. She seems to like talking to my mother, but then she turns to me. "He always told me he talked his way out of problems."

"I know. Apparently, Jason—the other guy—doesn't like to talk."

"He'll find plenty to talk about in prison," my mother says, her lips pressed together in disapproval.

Marilee called a couple of minutes ago and Quinn had passed on the fact that Jason had been arrested several blocks away from the shelter.

Once we finish talking about Jason, we just sit here.

I feel bad. The nurses certainly didn't make any promises to Mrs. Russo. I think she believes he might die.

"I never should have let him stay on at that shelter," Mrs. Russo mutters as she rummages in her purse for something. "I should have made him quit. He'd listen to me if I made him."

My mother reaches into her purse and gives the older woman one of those small packets of tissues. "Try not to worry. It's out of our hands."

I keep waiting for my mother to say more, but she doesn't, not even when Mrs. Russo starts to cry a little. I wish Marilee was here. She'd tell us all how to have faith and then she'd pray about the matter and—I never thought I'd wish for God to be in control of things, but I do now. This is all too big for me. I can't stand to see Mrs. Russo giving up and crying like that.

I feel the tears form in my eyes and I blink them away.

"Would anyone like something to drink?" I say. "There's a vending machine in the hall outside."

Mrs. Russo shakes her head.

"You go ahead though, dear," my mother says as she starts patting the older woman on her shoulder.

I nod and stand up. I think I'm going to break, but I walk to the hallway as fast as I can anyway. I need to find a wall.

The vending machine is in a corner at the end of the hallway. It's out of the way of things a little, and quiet here. I take a deep breath and lean against the side of the vending machine so I face the wall. If I clench my jaws and empty my mind, I think I can stop the breaking inside of me. I wish I knew some rules for a time like this. Mark can't die. It hasn't occurred to anyone yet, but I'll be responsible if he does. I'm the one who had to plan this whole prom banquet. Mark had been right that the kids weren't ready for it. And, look what happened. Mark might die because of it.

I swallow hard and keep staring at the wall. I can do this. It's all I know. If I can only stay in control of my tears, there's still a chance it won't all be so bad. I refuse to blink again because, if I do, I know a tear will roll down my cheeks. I'm Becca. I don't cry.

If I wasn't staring at the wall so hard, I probably would have heard the footsteps.

"Becca, is that you?"

I look up and there's Pastor Engstrom from Marilee's church. I knew he was coming, but I didn't think he'd see me like this.

"Is everything okay?" he asks.

"Oh, yeah, I was just—" I have to think a minute. "Getting some coffee."

"There's no coffee in the vending machine here."

"Oh, yeah, I realized that. I just—" I hiccup.

Then I hiccup again and I can't stop the tears. I close my mouth and try to clench my jaw, but there's another hiccup and I'm a mess.

The pastor uses his own dollar bill to get me a bottle of water out of the vending machine and he gives it to me,

"I'm not usually so—" I say and hiccup again.

"Don't worry about it," the pastor says as I drink some of the water. "It's a hard time."

I nod and take another drink of water.

"Have you prayed about the young man yet?" the pastor asks.

I shake my head and the tears start to fall in earnest

now. "I don't know how to pray. But you already know that. You know everything."

The pastor looks a little startled. "Did I miss something someplace?"

"It's just you sound like you know everything about me when you preach," I say. I try not to make my voice accusatory, but it sounds a little that way to me anyway.

The pastor grins. "Well, I can't take credit for that part of things. Jesus is the one who knows about you."

"Then He should do something about me and not just sit there."

Okay, so my tone of voice is not improving. I just don't think it's fair that this Jesus knows all of these things and then lets me make mistakes anyway. I could have used a clue that the prom banquet was going to end in a disaster.

"He does want to do something about you," the pastor says gently. "He's just waiting for you to give Him permission first."

That makes me cry even harder to think that Jesus is waiting for me. No one has ever waited for me. I've had to battle my way into every place in my life where I've wanted to be. Law school. Those little cliques in junior high. Even the Sisterhood; I was invited because of the cancer but it took me a long time to feel I belonged. I've never had anyone wait for me like the pastor says Jesus is waiting for me.

The pastor offers to talk to me about all of this in his study and I tell him I'll call him and make an appointment. I mean it, too.

Then we both look down the hall and I see the sisters coming toward me.

I wipe the tears off of my face and turn to the pastor. "Don't tell them I've been crying, okay?"

The pastor nods. "I always keep confidences."

"Good," I say as I walk toward the sisters. I can't wait to get them all praying. We fought death together before and we didn't know about praying back then. I feel better than I have since I heard Mark was stabbed. Jesus is waiting for me. How about that?

Chapter Seventeen

⤷ ⟋

"Take away love and our earth is a tomb."
—Robert Browning

Carly was the one who brought us this quote. She went through a poetry phase. I think it was her aunt's idea because she'd given Carly a book of love poetry one Christmas. All we had were these poetry quotes. It was enough to make me resign from the group, but Lizabett loved it and I could see Marilee tolerated it. Back then I vowed that, if I ever did fall in love, it wouldn't be one of those deep things that made me feel like I would die if something happened to my beloved. I already knew that lots of things could happen in life. I saw no reason to risk it all.

We're all sitting in the emergency room. My mother, Mrs. Russo, Pastor Engstrom, and the four of us sisters. Quinn stayed for a little bit and then he had to leave. The rest of us have settled into a whole row of chairs along the right side of the waiting room and I can see one of the nurses looks at us periodically as she walks through on her way to the back. I know we're taking up too much room, but there's still space for others to sit.

Besides, I think the others like having us there. They've asked Pastor Engstrom to come over and pray with them for the people they're here waiting for, too.

The last report we got on Mark was that he was still in surgery. They say they'll let Mrs. Russo go up and see him when he's well enough. But they caution us that it won't be until morning. In the meantime, they tell us not to worry, that things are going as well as they can.

Mrs. Russo says that there's no need for everyone to stay, but she says it in a small voice and no one makes a move to leave.

Lizabett asks to write in the journal and so I give her the notebook.

Hi, this is Lizabett. It makes me feel better to have something to do so I'm going to write in here. We're all so worried about Mark. I thought it was a fairy-tale evening—oh, you should have seen everyone dressed up like they were—it was beautiful. And then this. How could it end with Mark getting stabbed?

Becca has been crying, but she doesn't admit it and the rest of us are pretending we don't notice. Becca always thinks she's so tough, but I know better. I could tell earlier tonight that she cares about Mark. She will take it hard if he dies.

You would think that, as much as the Sisterhood has faced death, we would be better at it. But we're not. I'm just as scared as I would be if I didn't know any of the things that they can do for you in a hospital.

Oh, my—I look up and see dozens of kids standing outside the big window leading to the entryway to this room. I better put the journal away now.

This is Becca. Lizabett just handed the journal back to me. She has this funny look on her face and I follow her gaze to the window. Oh, my—it must be all of the kids from the shelter. I recognize Candice and Ricky and Lupe and—why, I think they're all here.

They're just standing outside the entry window though. I see one of the office clerks going back into her side office and she's obviously been out there telling them something.

I stand up. One of us needs to go and talk to them.

I open the door to the emergency room and step through the small hall and then the main door opens, and I'm outside in the darkness. The kids have formed a half-circle around the emergency-room door and, when I step through the last door, they all light the candles they are holding.

I recognize the candles from the candelabras we had on our tables earlier.

"He's not dead," I say quickly and in a hushed tone. They look like a funeral procession.

"We know he's not dead," Lupe says. "We all came to give blood."

I am struck with how different my life has been from theirs. I didn't even think of the need for blood. But they do. They've had friends get stabbed before.

"The candles are to show our support," Candice says. "We're going to stay here until he's better."

"I'm not sure—" I begin and then turn to see that Mrs. Russo has stepped through the door behind me.

"These are the kids?" she asks me.

I nod, but it's not necessary. They are obviously the kids her grandson may have given his life to help. I look at them and wish they looked more promising. They are a mismatched assortment. Some of the girls are still wearing their evening gowns and they're rumpled. Most of the guys have changed into their jeans and T-shirts and the T-shirts are wrinkled and there are holes here and there. We have black kids, white kids and Asians. None of the kids are smiling. There's not a poster child among them.

"How'd they get here?" Mrs. Russo asks as she looks around.

"We took the bus, ma'am," Candice says, and I'm glad her tone is respectful.

"The driver thought we were a gang and didn't want to let us on," Lupe adds. "But we talked to him and told him about Mr. Mark."

Mrs. Russo looks them over for a minute and they meet her eyes as she does. Finally, she reaches for her purse.

The woman hands me several hundred dollar bills. "They'll be hungry. Order them some hamburgers or something. Kids that age are always hungry. They may as well eat."

I stand there with my mouth open as Mrs. Russo turns to go back inside.

"Thank you," one of the guys calls out after her and then the kids break into quiet applause.

Mrs. Russo turns around and gives them a small smile. "You're welcome."

I end up sending four of the guys to a hamburger place that's down the street a little from the hospital. They're to bring back one hundred hamburgers and bottled waters to go around. I'm surprised that none of the guys who were not chosen made a fuss about it. I look at the kids as they place their orders with the four I'd picked. There doesn't seem to be any resentment or impatience. I think these kids finally became a team. Mark would be proud.

Which only reminds me that he's not here to see his kids come together like adults.

I go back inside to sit down. I'm not so sure I can act like an adult myself about now, either.

"She is a grandmother, after all," Lizabett says quietly after I explained what happened.

I nod. "She must be."

My hamburger has ketchup and pickles on it, but no mustard. Just the way I like it. Lupe put in my order and how she knew, I don't know. The buns are buttered and then grilled so I know Marilee will approve. She nods at me as she bites into her hamburger. Hers is on a whole-wheat bun. I don't know how the kids got to know the rest of us so quickly.

Even Mrs. Russo was happy with the cup of hot soup they brought for her.

When we've all eaten, there's nothing left to do but worry. At some point during the night, I take the journal out of my purse and just hold it. I don't even need to write in it. I like just feeling the paper under my fingers. Marilee was right about the journal. It has helped me to think about some things. I found the courage to talk to my mother about how she felt about adopting me. I'm going to tell her and my father a big thank you sometime soon. I made an appointment with Pastor Engstrom and I'm going to keep it. I feel like maybe I could get to know Jesus after all. Wouldn't that be something?

And Mark—what can I say about Mark?

I must doze off, just holding the Sisterhood journal, because the next thing I know Marilee is shaking me awake.

I open my eyes. It takes me a minute to remember where I am and what's going on.

"Easy," Marilee says as she keeps her hand on my arm. "He's going to be all right. The doctors just came to tell us that everything's going to be okay."

I can see Lizabett outside talking to the kids from the shelter so she must be telling them what Marilee just told me. I feel like the whole waiting room is taking a deep breath. I look over to say something to Mrs. Russo and notice she is gone.

"She went up to see Mark," my mother says. "She's going to come back and tell us all how he's doing."

I nod. I don't even notice that tears are rolling down my face until Marilee gives me a hug and wipes them away.

"Sorry about that," I say as I try to blink back some of the tears.

"I'm not," Marilee says as she gives my shoulders a final squeeze. "You're just showing your heart."

I start to protest that I don't have a heart, but then I shut my mouth. No one believes me anyway when I say that and, truthfully, I no longer believe it, either. I may not be a princess, but I'm not a Tin Man, either.

I guess I'm just Becca.

We all sit in the waiting room until Mrs. Russo comes back. Her face is flushed with satisfaction and she tells us that Mark is doing well.

"He asked to see you," Mrs. Russo says to me. "The nurse said you can't stay long, but you can go up and say hi."

Mrs. Russo gives me the room number and I head for the elevator. The hallways are brightly lit even though it's the middle of the night. I find Mark's room with no problem.

He's lying in a bed with bandages wrapped around his forehead and his chest. He has bruises on his face that make his earlier one look pale.

"You came," he says.

I step close to the bed. I can't seem to speak.

Mark holds out his hand to me.

I take it.

"I wanted to tell you that it's not your fault," he says.

I blink. "How did you know I'd think that?"

He tries to smile. "I'm getting to know you."

He squeezes my hand and I just stand there for a minute.

"Were they praying for me? Marilee and Quinn?" Mark finally asks.

"Yes."

"Good. I told God I was going to give that church a chance if I made it."

I nod. "Me, too."

"We'll go together."

I nod. That sounds good to me.

A nurse stops in the doorway and tells me my time is up.

"Come see me later?" Mark asks.

"Of course."

Mark's first visit back at the shelter is Thursday. I've taken an additional week off from my internship so I could cover some of Mark's duties while he's been in the hospital and then at his grandmother's recovering. The judge looked at me funny when I asked for the extra week, but, when I explained why I needed more time, she told me she thought I'd made the right decision. Life wasn't all about the law.

The old Becca would never have considered stepping back from her law school commitments so she could help someone. I didn't even ask the judge if the extra week I took would affect her opinion of me when it came to future opportunities. I just knew I had to do it. For the kids at the shelter. For Mark. And, maybe most of all, for myself.

I'm not completely sure how to explain it all, but I make an attempt at the Sisterhood meeting that night. We're sitting at our table in the Pews and rewinding some stray lengths of yarn.

"Someone needed to step in and help," I say to the Sisterhood.

"And you have a heart," Lizabett adds.

I frown as I rewind some of that ugly beige yarn I was using earlier. I'd completely picked apart the scarf I was knitting and now I'm rolling up the yarn.

"No," I say. "It's just that Mark was hurt and I didn't want him to worry about what was happening at the shelter when he should just be thinking about getting well."

"Then you have a boyfriend, too," Lizabett adds.

I wind that beige yarn into a tight ball. I've decided there's no need to use ugly yarn. Not with all of the beautiful colors in the world. I'm going to donate this ball of yarn to a cat owner for their pet to play with.

"I think so." I grin as I answer Lizabett's question.

"But what about law school?" Carly asks.

"I can be flexible," I say. "Mark knows how it is to be in law school. He said we'd work it out."

I already talked to my parents about me becoming a Christian and we decided we'd work that out, as well. I can still celebrate the holidays with them.

We don't get much knitting done after I make my announcement. Instead, we talk about what we're going to do next. Carly is going to be taking more classes at PCC, Marilee is going to coach a girls' softball team, I'm going to finish up my internship with the judge, and Lizabett is going to inherit the journal.

"Really?" Lizabett says when I make the offer.

"I think it's time it goes to you," I say.

"Wow, I never thought it would ever get to me," Lizabett says.

It's not easy for Lizabett to be the youngest one.

I reach into my bag and pull out the journal. "Use it in good health."

"Remember, you tell the story of all of us," Marilee says.

"Try not to use too many staples," Carly adds. "The thing will already set off the metal detector in an airport."

"I'll guard it with my life," Lizabett says and I think she's only half kidding.

I would say something, but I suddenly realize I would do the same. The journal has become important to me, too. I can't wait to see what Lizabett writes now that it's her turn.

"Hey," she says. "Do you think it would set off a metal detector if I took it on a trip to Paris someday?"

"If you're taking a trip to Paris with that in your purse, I'll personally remove all of the staples and replace them with tape," Carly says.

Lizabett grins. "If I don't go to Paris, I might start my own business."

"Really?" I say. "What?"

"Planning weddings," Lizabett says as though daring us to say something discouraging.

"You can do anything," I say and the others nod in agreement. "Anything at all."

We spend a little extra time together tonight. It's like we've run a great race and need to rest a bit together before we take any more steps. Uncle Lou brings us each an extra cup of tea and we just sit together for a while.

* * * * *

Dear Reader,

I thought long and hard as I got ready to tell Becca's story. Each of the young women in the Sisterhood of the Dropped Stitches is unique, but Becca is the one who has been the most wounded by the experience of having cancer. She is the one who has fought the disease and hasn't been able to give up her armor even though she is no longer in danger.

I have known many Beccas in my life and, in some ways, I am part Becca, too. It is easy to defend ourselves so well that we don't let any emotions out. I tried to show the thawing that was necessary in Becca's heart to be truly healed. It is the same softening that needs to take place in many of our hearts.

Becca had some good friends to help her acknowledge her emotions. If you are like Becca, I hope and pray that you have some good friends, as well. If you don't have a good friend, I have found that local churches are a good place to look for one.

I'd love to hear from you once you have read Becca's story. I always like to hear what my readers have to say. You can reach me at my Web site, www.janettronstad.com., or you can write to me in care of Steeple Hill Books, 233 Broadway, Suite 1001 New York, NY 10279.

Sincerely,

Janet Tronstad

lois FiNis 4/13/10 Im afraid I wasn't much interested in this, not sure why.

QUESTIONS FOR DISCUSSION

1. When the other members of the Sisterhood first met Becca as teenagers, they thought she was heartless. Becca herself said later that she couldn't afford to give in to her emotions. Why do you think she felt this way?

2. Everyone deals with hardship in different ways. When bad things such as sickness or tragedy happen to you, how do you deal with them?

3. All of the Sisterhood of the Dropped Stitches members wondered how God could let them have cancer. What questions do you have for God when you look at the hard times in your own life? Why do you think God lets some people have cancer?

4. When you experience hard times, what is the most helpful thing your friends can do for you? What ways did her friends help Becca deal with feelings in this book?

5. Becca also had problems expressing her appreciation to her adoptive parents. Why do you think she felt as if she couldn't thank them? Do you ever feel that a simple thank-you isn't enough and end up not saying anything?

6. Becca had a hard time acknowledging that the girls at the shelter were important to her. Can you think

of a similar time in your own life when you didn't want to admit that someone was important to you?

7. All of the sisters felt that they had missed out on important parts of teenage life. Do you feel that you missed out on various stages in your life? How have you made your peace with what you've missed?

8. Do you think the Sisters were able to experience some of what they missed as teenagers by helping the teenagers from the shelter plan a prom-like banquet? Have you ever done something similar?

9. Becca tried to control her life by following the rules. Do you try to control you life? In what ways? What happens when you try to control your life?

10. Which of the Sisters in the book is most like you? Why?

11. The Sisters each have different personalities. Do you think they would have become friends if they hadn't had cancer together? Think of your friends. Are you and your friends alike or different? Does that make the friendship better?

12. Becca didn't like writing in the journal at first. Why do you think it was hard for her? How do you think Lizabett will do writing in the journal?

You could
WIN
the
Dropped Stitches Heart!

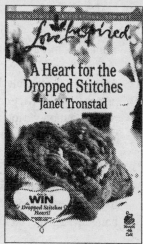

The Love Inspired series is giving away the 10-inch knitted heart featured on the cover of A Heart for the Dropped Stitches, and you could be the lucky winner!

To enter the Dropped Stitches Heart Sweepstakes, *visit*

www.WinTheDroppedStitchesHeart.com

or mail

IN THE U.S.: 3010 Walden Ave., P.O. Box 9069, NY 14269-9069
IN CANADA: 225 Duncan Mill Road, Don Mills, ON M3B 3K9

Name _____ (PLEASE PRINT)

Address _____ Apt. #

City _____ State/Prov. _____ Zip/Postal Code

REQUEST YOUR FREE BOOKS!

2 FREE INSPIRATIONAL NOVELS
PLUS 2
FREE
MYSTERY GIFTS

Love Inspired.

YES! Please send me 2 FREE Love Inspired® novels and my 2 FREE mystery gifts (gifts are worth about $10). After receiving them, if I don't wish to receive any more books, I can return the shipping statement marked "cancel". If I don't cancel, I will receive 4 brand-new novels every month and be billed just $4.24 per book in the U.S. or $4.74 per book in Canada, plus 25¢ shipping and handling per book and applicable taxes, if any*. That's a savings of over 20% off the cover price! I understand that accepting the 2 free books and gifts places me under no obligation to buy anything. I can always return a shipment and cancel at any time. Even if I never buy another book, the two free books and gifts are mine to keep forever.

113 IDN ERXA 313 IDN ERWX

Name	(PLEASE PRINT)	
Address		Apt. #
City	State/Prov.	Zip/Postal Code

Signature (if under 18, a parent or guardian must sign)

Order online at www.LoveInspiredBooks.com

Or mail to Steeple Hill Reader Service:

IN U.S.A.: P.O. Box 1867, Buffalo, NY 14240-1867
IN CANADA: P.O. Box 609, Fort Erie, Ontario L2A 5X3

Not valid to current subscribers of Love Inspired books.

Want to try two free books from another series?
Call 1-800-873-8635 or visit www.morefreebooks.com

* Terms and prices subject to change without notice. N.Y. residents add applicable sales tax. Canadian residents will be charged applicable provincial taxes and GST. Offer not valid in Quebec. This offer is limited to one order per household. All orders subject to approval. Credit or debit balances in a customer's account(s) may be offset by any other outstanding balance owed by or to the customer. Please allow 4 to 6 weeks for delivery. Offer available while quantities last.

Your Privacy: Steeple Hill Books is committed to protecting your privacy. Our Privacy Policy is available online at www.SteepleHill.com or upon request from the Reader Service. From time to time we make our lists of customers available to reputable third parties who may have a product or service of interest to you. If you would prefer we not share your name and address, please check here. ☐

LIREG08R

Love Inspired®

TITLES AVAILABLE NEXT MONTH

Don't miss these four stories in August

HER PERFECT MAN by Jillian Hart
The McKaslin Clan
New neighbor Chad Lawson seems too perfect. At least to
Rebecca McKaslin, who's been burned by Prince Charming
before. Yet, as Rebecca gets to know Chad, his reliable, friendly
nature challenges her resistance to relationships. Maybe God put
him in her life for a reason.

LONE STAR SECRET by Lenora Worth
Homecoming Heroes
David Ryland is about to fly his final military mission. Then
he must face up to his past. His family was a mystery until his
father confessed his parentage in a deathbed letter. A letter that
Anna Terenkov knows *all* about. If David can open his heart to
the truth, will he find room for Anna?

HIDDEN TREASURES by Kathryn Springer
All work and no play is Cade Halloway's motto. His new
project: selling his family's vacation home. Yet Cade must wait
until after his sister's wedding. And deal with photographer
Meghan McBride. But what Cade doesn't know is that love is
just one of many surprises to be discovered on the property!

BLUEGRASS HERO by Allie Pleiter
Kentucky Corners
Dust-covered cowboys are the norm at Gil Sorrent's ranch. Until
a visit to Emily Montague's bath shop has them cleaning up their
acts. Now they spend more time courting than working. Gil is
determined to give Emily a piece of his mind, but it's his heart
she's after.